MY FOREVER COWBOY

DIANE J. REED

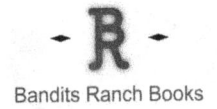

Bandits Ranch Books

Copyright © 2017 by Diane J. Reed
All rights reserved.
No part of this book may be reproduced in any form or by any electronic or mechanical means, including information storage and retrieval systems, without written permission from the author, except for the use of brief quotations in a book review.

Cover design by Najla Qamber at Najla Qamber Designs, www.najlaqamberdesigns.com

1

"My Forever Cowboy, can I help you?"

Avery twirled a blue pen between her fingers, customized with her lipstick-red business name and cowboy-hat logo, as she waited for the caller to make a request for her commercial photography studio.

"I'm Dixie Jackson at the Stampede Cards & Gifts headquarters in Denver. Am I speaking to the owner?"

"Yes, this is Avery Smart."

"Well, Ms. Smart, your cowboy calendar last year turned out to be our biggest seller in Colorado. And we'd like to commission you to produce another one for all our stores across the country as well as our website. Naturally, we'd want an exclusive contract. Would that be possible?"

"Exclusive? Can you explain what you mean by that?"

"Certainly. We'd like twelve images of new cowboys for a calendar that's sold nowhere else but Stampede, and we're prepared to pay a premium. I don't know where you find them, Ms. Smart," Dixie gushed, "but those cowboys in your calendar last year are the best-looking men we've ever seen! So rugged yet sincere, like a young John Wayne. Customers tell us they want to throw their arms around these men and ride off into a sunset. Could you find a dozen new cowboys like that for an exclusive Stampede calendar?"

Avery swallowed hard, slipping a lock of her long, copper hair behind her ear. "Of course!" she replied, her acorn-brown eyes narrowing as marbles ricocheted in her stomach. She drew a deep breath to slow her heartbeat.

This was the hard part—

Time to seal the deal.

Avery's anxiety always spiked at moments like this, when she was forced to transform herself into an Ice Queen and demand what she was worth—and then some. She'd worked her butt off for five years to build up this business, and she knew her success depended on two things: raw talent and pure guts. Swiftly, she scribbled her terms on a notepad, adding an extra ten percent just to prove she had moxie. Then she went for it.

"You realize that to produce a calendar with new cowboy images for only Stampede, my rates would have to be…tripled. Up front. And I insist on my studio logo being featured prominently on the calendar as well as receiving…sixty percent…of the profits."

"Deal," Dixie agreed faster than Avery could blink. "Congratulations, Ms. Smart. You've just gone nationwide!"

Avery glanced in shock across the room at her assistant Shae, who was filing her long pink fingernails and applying tiny, black buckaroo stickers to the edges. Startled, Shae met her gaze and punched the speaker button on the office phone at her desk, tilting forward to listen to the conversation.

"Tripled rates and sixty-percent profit on the calendar it is," Dixie confirmed. "My one stipulation is that you supply all images to us within three weeks. We ship calendars to our stores in the fall, and we need the images ahead of time for promo. Will that work for you, Ms. Smart?"

"Absolutely," Avery lied in a silvery tone, staring at Shae with abject panic in her eyes. "I'll send you the contract and invoice right away, and you'll have your images within three weeks."

"Thank you!" Dixie trilled. "It's such a pleasure to feature your cowboys in our product line. It must be wonderful to photograph all those brawny men who were born to forge frontiers and win the hearts of women," she sighed wistfully. "They look so loyal, with that twinkle in their eyes that says they'll be yours *forever*."

Right, forever—as sincere as Satan himself, Avery thought. Because it's all a lie, sold through expert marketing.

The truth was, Avery had never met a "forever cowboy" in her life—without a price. She'd grown up in Bandits Hollow, Colorado, an old western town in the Rocky Mountains historically famous for hiding outlaws. And she'd seen first hand the way most girls from her high school had gotten their hearts shattered by love 'em and leave 'em cowboys. Or worse, thrown away their career aspirations to chase good-looking guys in Stetsons and spurs with big rodeo dreams, only to discover that they'd lost their identities along the way. That was never going to happen to Avery—she was determined to be her own woman. Yet her knack for choosing exactly the right cowboys who appeared as hot and loyal as every woman's fantasy had vaulted her into one of the fastest-growing commercial photography studios in Colorado. It didn't hurt that the cowgirl-bohemian fashion trend was all the rage, and advertising firms as far away as Fort Collins were demanding a constant stable of handsome cowboys as backdrops for their ad campaigns. Avery's timing couldn't have been better.

"Well, Dixie," Avery concluded their conversation, "I'm thrilled you love our unique brand of sexy and sincere cowboys. We'll be in touch soon," she promised. "Have a My Forever Cowboy day!"

Avery hung up the receiver and sank her head into her hands.

"Oh Shae, what have I done?" she moaned. "You heard her! She wants twelve photos of new cowboys in *three weeks*. Who look rugged and loyal to the bone, of course. Do you have any idea how hard that is to find? Even if it is make believe?"

"All the more dates for me!" Shae giggled, fluttering her fingers and admiring the buckaroo decals on her nails. "Besides, MFC will make a *ton* more money now that it's gone national. So tell me, should I wear a black minidress and boots to go with these nails, or more of a neon-pink rodeo ensemble? I love scouting for new cowboys!" Shae grinned, her smile making her sweet face all the more adorable, framed by blonde, curly hair and sparkly pink eyeshadow that matched her lips. But then her glossy mouth fell into a pout. "Too bad I never manage to keep any of them."

"Oh Shae, we've been over this," Avery sighed, tapping her pen and glancing out her office window at the downtown buildings of Colorado Springs. "You grew up in a suburb here, not way out on a ranch like me. Take it from a veteran of Bandits Hollow, there are only two types of forever cowboys. One is hot and sexy, rides bulls or broncs, and is great for one-night stands pretty much forever—even if he's married to somebody else. But if you want to see him more than once a year, you'll have to follow him on the rodeo circuit, shine his spurs, and put up with all of his other…shall we say… dalliances? Before he finally breaks a hip or his back and needs a full-time nurse, of course. The second type of forever cowboy is over forty and has a paunch, owns land three hours from *anywhere*, and will be loyal to you to kingdom come if you move to *his* ranch, attend *his* grandma's church and punt out at least three of *his* kids—with no time off for good behavior."

"Can't you find one that's *both*?" Shae asked, looking dejected. "You know, sexy and loyal?"

"There's no such thing!" Avery shook her head, knowing that hot-to-trot Shae had blistered through nearly all of the cowboys in her studio arsenal, and she was running out of inventory.

"Why not?" Shae protested, appearing miffed. "Maybe we just need to try harder. You know, beat the sagebrush a little more."

Avery leaned forward on her elbows and stared intently at Shae to make her point. "Repeat after me: hot, sexy cowboys don't abandon their thrill-seeking ways to move to the suburbs to be cabana boys, mix fruity drinks, and service young women's needs. Alpha, Shae—they're all alpha! Sure, you may dress like the sweetheart of the rodeo, but unless you feel like giving up your family and friends and that shopping mall you're addicted to, you're dreaming. This is more than country-line dancing at the Saddle Swap Bar and then going back to your old life. Cowboys always want you to give up everything," she paused with a fragile crack in her voice, "and then they *leave*. Got it? So I suggest you have as good a time as you can until the right kind of forever comes along. Which won't be a cowboy."

"But I hate paunchy! I'm too young for a guy who isn't fit. By the way, today's nail base color is hot pink," she insisted, holding up her bottle of polish. "It wouldn't kill you to spend a little more time on upkeep. As in, look approachable for a change? I have enough polish to do all of your nails—both hands and feet."

Avery glanced down at her neutral-beige nails that coordinated with her crisply-tailored, ivory blazer and skirt, specifically designed to keep rough and ready cowboys *away*, not attract them. She rolled her eyes.

"Cowboys are the drug, and I'm the pusher," Avery stated flatly. "I hate to be so blunt, Shae, but really smart dealers never indulge in their own dope. They simply deliver the goods and make the cash. And I make *very* good cash, as you know, because it pays your wages."

A wry smile surfaced on Shae's lips. "Are you trying to convince *me* of that, or yourself? I've seen the way you look at some of the hot guys we approach at rodeos for photographs. Don't try and tell me you're immune."

"Nobody's immune—that's the point! Cowboys are pure heroin. They make you feel giddy and beautiful, like you're the center of their whole world, until the very moment they stop. And then everything you thought was real comes crashing down at your feet. Women like me don't have time for that kind of free fall. We have to keep our businesses afloat and pay our employees. Like you."

Avery shook her head, marveling at the differences between her and her assistant. Although only five years separated them, she felt a million years older than 21-year-old Shae, who still had enough emotional baby fat to think it was fun to paint her nails, dance at cowboy bars, and shop at malls for fake silver buckles and cowgirl boots made in Taiwan. At 26, Avery *had* to make a good living. Everything about her life rested solely on her firm shoulders. She'd been virtually on her own since she was sixteen after her father died, without the parental safety net that Shae had, enabling Shae to party all night and still have a soft place to land at the condo she rented cheap from her parents. But Shae was as dependable as she was boy crazy, always helpful with props during photo shoots and diligent about updating accounts—as long as she applied a fresh coat of nail polish every morning. Best of all, Shae was willing to travel any distance for photo shoots of cowboys, even at the drop of a hat.

"Well, sweetie, if it's new cowboys you want," Avery assured her, staring at a website on her computer, "you're in luck. Because we have a mighty big job to find a dozen of them pronto. From the looks of this Colorado rodeo schedule, the only event for tomorrow, June twentieth, is…oh crap!"

Avery typed furiously on her keyboard, searching several other websites at the click of her mouse. Her shoulders drooped.

"Seriously? There are no other rodeos this weekend except for Outlaw Days in Bandits Hollow?"

"Ooh!" replied Shae. "We've never been to that one. I'm game if you are. What's with the scrunchy face all of a sudden? You afraid to go home?"

"No," Avery protested too quickly, her eyebrows knit together. "It's just that, well, we'll need to stop in to check on my mom. She's a rather feeble widow, and," Avery hesitated, choosing her words carefully, "she has some…eccentricities." She peered over the monitor at Shae with a vulnerable look in her eyes. "Not everyone can handle dealing with her, if you know what I mean."

"Fine by me!" Shae grinned. "I'll bring her some chocolate broncos." She fished inside her desk drawer and seized a bag of candy. "Everybody loves these. They're from the new chocolate shop that went up two blocks from here." Shae stood to her feet and grabbed her suede-fringed purse from the back of her chair, slinging the strap over her shoulder. "C'mon, boss, we need to get packing. We've got a road trip ahead—time to shop for cowboys!"

"Not just any cowboys. *Forever* cowboys," Avery corrected. "It's not enough for them to look tough. They have to seem like the kind of men who might stay."

"I know, I know," conceded Shae, impatient with Avery's familiar instructions. "Don't worry, you can count on me to get the number of anybody who comes close to fitting that bill." She fetched a stack of MFC business cards from her desk and stuffed them in her purse. "As long as you keep letting *me* make the follow-up calls to all those handsome wranglers," she said with a wink. "Even if they don't stick around forever."

2

She moved in shadows...
Evangeline Tinker picked her way carefully through the moist, dense foliage beneath the cool pine boughs at dawn.

She was no stranger to this raw, wild country.

High up in the Rocky Mountains at 9,000 feet, the wilderness edge of Bandits Hollow was a land she returned to every June to collect her herbs and wildflowers. It was on the summer solstice at sunrise that wild rose, Indian paintbrush, and columbine held the most potency for...

Magic.

But Evangeline never called it that.

To her, it was simply the current of life. A flow as easy as a river, or as deadly, depending on how you looked at it.

As she drew a lock of long gray hair away from her face that had been known to transfix many with her extraordinary beauty, even in old age, Evangeline leaned closer to examine a healthy stand of St. John's Wort. She smiled at its yellow flowers as though they were friends. Dear cohorts in a life spent helping others to find their way, to find themselves, and most of all, to find…

Love.

For it was a lack of love that Evangeline knew could shrivel a soul most. And as a descendent of a long line of Irish Travelers, it had been her mission to help others revive their faith in being led by the heart. Naturally, Evangeline used the herbal lore that had been handed down to her in a leather-bound book she'd inherited from her ancestors in the old country. Her mind was an encyclopedia of botanicals, potions, omens, and spells, as well as a repository of the time-honored wisdom she'd received from her forebears. But there was one thing only Bandits Hollow could offer.

And as Evangeline stepped toward a pale shaft of early morning light that sliced through the trees, she saw it.

The fairy slipper.

An exquisite wildflower, with dewy lavender petals that shimmered in the light. They framed an extended lip petal that featured a patch of yellow, as bright as the sun.

Evangeline's breath hitched.

It took a lot to startle her in old age. Yet the sight of this rare orchid, which only grew in the Rocky Mountains between 7,000-10,000 feet, always took her breath away.

In silence, she gazed for a moment at its delicate beauty. This annual reunion was sacred to her, deep within a secret grove that she kept tucked inside her heart. She drew a long breath and smiled.

"Good mornin', my dear," she said in her Appalachian

accent, forged from a hard-scrabble childhood in a region of the country called Bender Lake, which most city folk branded as hillbilly territory. "So nice to see you again."

Evangeline pulled a vial from the pocket of her ankle-length, velvet black dress and withdrew a pair of pewter scissors with handles in the shape of a swan. She stepped up to the fairy slipper and lovingly ran her fingers along its light purple petals. Then, oh-so-carefully, without tugging or shaking the endangered plant, she snipped off several long petals and cradled them in her palm.

"Thank you," she whispered to the flower with a nod. She crouched down on her crimson, lace-up granny boots and gazed at the plant with rapt attention, as though listening to its murmurs. At that moment, the flower began to shiver in a warm breeze, peculiar for that hour of the morning. The gentle caress of air made goosebumps alight on Evangeline's skin. She stood to her feet, watching the fairy slipper tremble. Then she lifted her gaze to an opening in the pine boughs and spied an old homestead off in the distance. The wooden sign that hung from the timber frame over the dirt entrance road was slowly swinging in the breeze. The sign said *Lazy C Ranch*.

Evangeline Tinker began to laugh, her eerie cackle echoing through the trees.

"My, oh my," she smiled, revealing a gold front tooth, "I do believe somebody's about to fall in love."

She stroked the petals in her hand, observing that one of them had a slight split at the end. When she brought the edges together, she pressed a drop of pine sap that had fallen from the trees to her palm and fused the petal to make it look whole. "And I reckon there's gonna be one hell of a reunion soon."

Evangeline opened her small glass vial and placed the petals inside, sealing it with a cork. "There," she said, nodding at a great horned owl that was perched on a branch nearby. She met the bird's gaze and watched its yellow eyes flare. The owl spread its massive wings and called to her before departing in the direction of the old homestead.

"Yes indeedy," Evangeline confirmed to the owl, slipping the vial inside her dress pocket. "It's high time we visited our ol' friend Jubilee."

3

Evangeline Tinker's cackle filled the rustic dining room in the old homestead, making the china in a nearby hutch clatter. She sat across a table from a plump woman with gray curls pulled back into a bun, who was wearing a brown calico dress that looked like it had been handed down by pioneers. The woman's chicory-blue eyes twinkled.

"That has to be the funniest dang thing I ever heard!" she burst, her ample tummy jiggling from laughter. "You actually told a woman to put stinging nettles in her husband's underwear to keep him from cheating?"

"I did no such thing, Jubilee." Evangeline wagged a finger at her. "You know perfectly well I *never* tell a body what to do."

"Well, I'm sure you *implied* it would work," Jubilee corrected, arching a brow. "So did it?"

"Did what?" Evangeline appeared innocent all of a sudden.

"Did the stinging nettles keep his piper in his pocket, if you know what I mean?"

Evangeline's lips curled into a smile. "All I know is that she never returned to my wagon at Bender Lake again."

"I'd say that's proof positive," Jubilee noted. "Oh, how I wish I could go to your Traveller's wagon any old time I had a problem," she mused, grabbing the teapot on the rough-hewn log table and pouring her friend a cup of tea. "You always seem to know the right thing to tell folks. Take my grandson Grant Hollow, for example." She pointed to a picture in a pine frame on a dresser of a strikingly handsome cowboy accepting a check the size of her dining room table while smiling for the camera. "He may win everything in sight in professional bull riding, but danged if he can keep a girl. If you ask me, he seems a bit lonely for female company. That's why he comes to visit me every summer while the pro tour is on break. He claims it's to help his old grandma with her ranch, but I've seen the way he gobbles up my home cooking and lingers around the fireplace to chat, his eyes marked by a faraway look, like there's some kind of hole inside him. Of course, he'd never admit any of that."

"Well, life on the road can be mighty difficult," Evangeline affirmed. In that moment, her timber-wolf gray eyes with golden flecks in the middle appeared weary.

"I suppose you oughta know, with your life as a Traveler. Think you could give me a little advice? A spell or two that might help him settle down?"

"In this old shack?" Evangeline's face crinkled into a grin. "Named after Clyde Hollow, the laziest rancher in the West?"

"That was over a hundred years ago!" Jubilee defended.

"My great-great grandpa was an outstanding train robber with the Bandits Hollow Gang, thank you very much. It wasn't his idea to get strung up by a vengeful posse. If Virgil Hollow hadn't taken in Clyde's son Nathaniel and raised him as his own to keep this ranch going, my family would've lost this land a long time ago, in case you forgot."

Evangeline grew quiet.

"No," she said softly. "I don't reckon I could ever… forget…such things."

The two women glanced at a framed wanted poster on the wall, featuring a sepia-toned photo of the Bandits Hollow Gang in the nineteenth century. In the center was a devastatingly handsome cowboy with a shock of dark hair and the name Virgil Hollow printed beneath his image. On his right stood a Native American man in a black coat and flat-brimmed hat, identified as Iron Feather. Beside Iron Feather was a young man whose head was tilted in a bemused expression, as if he didn't have a care in the world, marked as Clyde Hollow. But on Virgil Hollow's left side was an unnamed woman of breathtaking beauty in a long, Victorian dress who had her arm linked in his. Though young with a daring look in her eye, she had an uncanny resemblance to…

Evangeline Tinker.

"Oh criminy!" Jubilee yelped, darting her gaze out the dining room window. "Here comes my grandson Grant walking up the dirt road now." She reached across the table and seized Evangeline's hands in hers, peering into her eyes. "Ain't no one ever seen you here but me, honey. And you ain't got time to get away. So from here on out, I'll just refer to you as…my old friend Granny T. Okey-dokey?"

Evangeline nodded slowly.

When she pulled her hands free from Jubilee and turned from the table to look through the dining room window, Evangeline's eyes received a shock. The tall, strapping man approaching the homestead with hair as dark as night and eyes as piercing blue as the Rocky Mountain sky was the spitting image of…

Virgil Hollow.

And he held a wailing calf in his arms.

"Woman trouble, huh?" Evangeline withdrew the small vial from her dress pocket and held it up to show Jubilee. Inside, the purple fairy slipper petals quivered. "I must say, I got a distinct feelin' that won't be a problem much longer. But only if he picks a girl who's secretly got as much renegade in her as he does—and who'll do anything for those she loves."

"Really?" Jubilee clapped her hands together. "Oh, to see my grandson finally happy would make me shine from the inside out. When's it gonna happen? Who is she? I heard once that fairy slipper orchids are the world's most powerful aphrodisiac—"

"Now, now," Evangeline scolded. She tucked the vial back inside her pocket and folded her arms with a twinkle in her eyes. "You of all people know that I've never been one to reveal my methods."

4

Without so much as a knock, the front door flung open wide with a loud thump as though it had been kicked. Grant Hollow burst inside the homestead and set the calf down on the kitchen floor. The young animal managed to hold a shaky stance before glancing around the kitchen and releasing a mournful wail.

"Good morning, Grandma!" A smile lit up Grant's face, in spite of his dark, brooding good looks. "Don't worry about this little fella. He got cut with a bit of barbed wire while tangling with your south-side fence. From all his bawling, you'd think it was the end of the world."

Grant headed over to a cabinet beneath the kitchen sink and retrieved a bottle of alcohol and a rag along with a tin of Bag Balm. When the calf attempted to skitter away, he hoisted it up in his arms and set it smack dab on the kitchen table.

"Once I clean him up and get ointment on his surface scrapes, he'll be as good as new."

"Where are your bags?" Jubilee sighed, like Grant's behavior in her kitchen was par for the course. "All you got is your coat, honey."

"Who needs luggage when there's plenty of old clothes around here?" Grant teased her. "You never throw away a darn thing, Grandma. No worries," he smirked, "I got a duffle bag in the back of my truck by the road. Now sit still," he warned the calf, pinning its legs with his muscular left arm while he dabbed its wounds with alcohol. The calf launched into a high-pitched cry. "It's okay, buddy," Grant assured him, dipping his finger into the Bag Balm. He gently smoothed a line of ointment along a scrape on the calf's hip and leg. "We're almost done."

Grant scanned the calf thoroughly for any other cuts, dabbing ointment on the last remaining spots. He caressed its forehead and whispered a few more soothing words as if the animal were a treasured family pet before gathering the calf into the security of his large arms. Carefully, he set him on the floor in the direction of the open front doorway and stretched out his arms. The calf wobbled for a moment, blinking its eyes, then bolted out the homestead as fast as he could muster, galloping to rejoin the herd.

"There," said Grant, wiping his hands on his jeans. "I'm starving! You got any breakfast left?" When his gaze settled on the women in the dining room, he suddenly realized Jubilee had a guest.

"Oh, pardon me, ma'am," he said, removing his black cowboy hat and giving the stranger a nod. "Who's your friend, Grandma?" He tilted his head with a cocky smile. "And is there a reason you two are dressed like you've been in an episode of *Bonanza*?"

"Can't say you look any different," Jubilee replied with a smirk. "But if you must know, it was my turn to deliver homemade cinnamon rolls this year for the Outlaw Days community breakfast. Everybody in town is supposed to dress the part in full historical regalia to impress the tourists. You should've seen Dirk Meriwether in his mountain man outfit, complete with a cougar pelt over his shoulder. Half the kids in Bandits Hollow got a fright." She tucked her tennies further under her chair to hide the obvious anachronism and glanced up at Evangeline.

"Grant, this here is my old friend…Granny T."

"Pleased to meet you, ma'am," Grant said, walking over to the dining room with his hand outstretched. Evangeline kept her arms firmly folded.

"Best be washin' them hands first," she scolded, her eyes narrowing at the grime on his fingers.

"Oh, right." Grant checked his hand. He headed back to the kitchen and turned on the faucet at the sink. "Mind if I ask what the T stands for before I go to town to score one of Grandma's cinnamon rolls?" He rubbed his hands vigorously with a bar of soap and shot a glance at the women.

Jubilee stared wide-eyed across the table at her friend, unsure of exactly what to say.

Evangeline appeared unperturbed. "Why, everybody knows T stands for Trouble," she remarked lightly with a smile, her front gold tooth glinting in the window light. "Especially if you make a habit of poking your nose into other folks' business. Ain't most cowboys the silent sort who don't ask too many questions? Rest assured I'm happy to push the trouble part, honey, should you require any proof."

Evangeline's renowned cackle ripped through the homestead, making the plates in the dining room hutch clatter again. Quick as a flash, she turned and arrested Grant Hollow in a steel gaze, her timber-wolf eyes reminiscent of fractured ice, leaving even a veteran bull rider startled. This was a woman not to be messed with. "Now you'd best get along to town, cowboy," Evangeline's lips curled into a hint of a smile, "before your grandma's homemade cinnamon rolls grow cold."

5

When Avery and Shae rolled into Bandits Hollow in the late afternoon in Avery's white BMW convertible, they couldn't possibly have stood out more. The dusty old town looked liked it belonged in a western movie where squinty-eyed gunslingers stood on either side of the street with their hands over their hip holsters, ready for a shoot out.

"Wow," remarked Shae, rubbernecking at the vintage buildings and wooden boardwalks that lined the road, "guess we don't need props for ambience around here. Is that a donkey I see walking down the road?"

"Loose burros," sighed Avery as she parked in front of the Golden Wagon Hotel, a stately building decorated with period Victorian flourishes. "They used to be considered good luck charms by miners over a hundred years ago, not to mention that they pulled heavy carts, so now they're allowed to roam free. To appease the gold fairies, I guess." She ignored the animal that brazenly trotted up to her car and nuzzled her arm as if expecting treats. Digging into her blazer pocket, she pulled out a plastic bag and held it up for Shae. "Do you want to do the honors, or shall I?"

"Carrots?" Shae peered at the bag. "What do I do—set a few on my hand and whistle for him to come?"

"Not if you want to get out of this car without being stepped on. Turn around in your seat and throw the bag down the street as far as you can."

Confused, Shae grasped the bag and chucked the carrots with all her might, watching the burro race toward the bag.

"Ready, set, go!" commanded Avery, opening her door and dashing out the car. "Watch out for manure!"

Shae briskly followed suit, and in no time they were at the entrance to the Golden Wagon Hotel. Craning her neck, Shae took in the brick architecture with white molding that framed the building before her eyes settled on an old stagecoach by the door painted from top to bottom in gold. "Whoa," she observed, "this place seems rather…grand."

"Looks can be deceiving—and so can hotels," Avery said. "Back in the day, this used to be a brothel for gold miners. The town is called Bandits Hollow because this is where some famous outlaws used to hide out."

"Like Butch Cassidy and the Sundance Kid?"

"No, that was Hole-In-The-Wall, Wyoming," Avery replied. "Though Butch Cassidy did rob a bank in Telluride once." Avery pointed at a brass plaque next to the hotel door listing its historical attributes. "I used to work in the restaurant here when I was sixteen and had to rattle off these facts for tourists."

She paused for a moment, appearing to wrestle with difficult memories before reaching for the handle on the mahogany door. "Ever since I was old enough to make my own money, I've paid room and board for my mom in this hotel. She needed the support after my dad passed away."

"Support?" Shae said, tilting her head. "I don't mean to pry, but shouldn't *she* have been the one helping you, if you were only sixteen?"

Avery shrugged. "To be honest, she was never quite the same after my dad died. Like most cowboys, my dad couldn't stay away from rodeoing, even though my mom begged him to stop. It was like an addiction, something that made him feel alive on those rare days he had off from ranching. Money was always tight for us, and I guess it was the only thrill he got. He was eventually done in by a bronc in the Outlaw Days Rodeo, and that was the end of my family as I knew it." Avery's voice shook a little as she turned to Shae. "My mother's mind kind of snapped. He was her whole world—she didn't know anything else except being his wife. I had to grow up fast and become the sole bread winner."

"Oh my," Shae replied softly. "No wonder you don't like coming back for Outlaw Days."

"It's okay," Avery said in an unconvincing tone. "We do what we gotta do to make a buck, right?" She sucked in a breath and yanked open the hotel door. To her surprise, Shae seemed completely oblivious to the grand central staircase, crystal chandeliers, velvet Victorian wallpaper, and vintage rodeo posters that decorated the lobby of the hotel. Her gaze registered only one thing.

"Oh my God!" Shae squealed, her eyes sparkling like it

23

was Christmas day. "This place is crawling with cowboys! Good-looking ones, too. Blonde hair, red, jet black—there's a flavor for everybody!"

"We'll get to that, sweetie," smiled Avery, grateful that her assistant could be counted on for enthusiasm, even after a long drive. "Outlaw Days is a big deal in this county and it brings the cowboys out of the woodwork. We're lucky there were still rooms left. Let me stop in and check on my mom, then we'll fetch something to eat in the restaurant. After that, I promise you can gawk all you want—even score some phone numbers if you're brave enough. C'mon cowboy catcher, follow me."

Avery led the way up the grand staircase that ascended to the second floor, listening to Shae stumble on the steps behind her because she couldn't stop drooling at the swarm of men in the lobby with Stetson and Resistol hats who were there for the rodeo. When Avery made it to the top and turned down a hall, she headed to the last door on the right and halted. Its brass numbers said 13.

"Thirteen, huh?" Shae noted, fidgeting a little. "This room wouldn't be…haunted…would it?"

"You could call it that," Avery answered matter-of-factly. "But my mother's the guilty party who brought the ghost. She, um…she doesn't actually *believe* my dad's gone. Which means," Avery issued a short cough, "she talks to him. A *lot*." She knocked hard on the door and turned to Shae. "Don't worry, you get used to it."

"Come in!" called a bright voice from the other side. Avery turned the nob and entered a dimly-lit room, smiling at a cheerful woman in a white uniform with a name tag that said *June*. She stood beside an older woman in a wheelchair with gray, disheveled hair and a lost look in her eyes. All around the room were framed photos of a dark-haired man in a black cowboy hat riding broncs, roping cows, and wrestling steers. Between the pictures were shelves displaying trophies, belt buckles, and even saddle blankets marked with the places and names of the rodeo events he'd won. In the corner next to a window was an old saddle on a stand with the words *Emmet Smart, All-Around Cowboy* tooled prominently into the leather. The room looked like a dusty museum to his memory.

"Hi Mom!" Avery said with forced gaiety, giving the seated woman a wave.

Her mother merely squinted. "That you, Avery? What on earth do you have that silly suit on for? You can't go to Outlaw Days wearing white—you'll get filthy!"

"This is your *mother*?" Shae whispered discretely. "She looks old enough to be your…"

"Grandma, I know," Avery replied in a low tone. "The sad thing is she's only forty-six, but her mental state has made her deteriorate. That's why I pay June to look after her."

Avery walked up to the woman in the white uniform and smiled, giving her a hug. She kneeled beside her mother in the wheelchair.

"Doggone it," Avery mentioned kindly, looking into her mother's eyes. "I *would* look ridiculous at Outlaw Days in this outfit, huh? Good thing I came by and got your advice. Don't know what I'd do without you, Mom." She gave Shae a wink.

Her mother nodded self-righteously and fished for a crumpled photo from the pocket of her peach rodeo shirt appliquéd with yellow lariats. "Glad I mentioned it," she asserted, gazing with pride at the photo in her hand of a dashing cowboy in his mid-thirties before she held it up. "What would your father say if he saw you looking like a city slicker at Outlaw Days? Downright blasphemy."

Avery nodded in agreement. "Yep, I'm sure he'd be beside himself. Luckily, I brought some jeans and boots in my suitcase. So Mom, my friend Shae is here with me today—she's going to our rodeo for the first time. Shae, this is Pearl Smart."

"Pleased to meet you," Shae said. She withdrew the bag of chocolates from her purse. "We brought some candy for you from Colorado Springs. Freshly made."

Pearl peered at the bronco shapes of the chocolate and smiled. "Would you look at that, Emmett," she beamed at her photo. "Bet those are tasty!"

Avery's cheeks turned red at her remarks to the two-dimensional image.

"This is my husband Emmett," Pearl insisted to Shae. "Ain't he a handsome one? You might see him in an event tomorrow."

"Uh, okay," Shae replied politely, shooting a nervous look at Avery. "Guess I'll be on the lookout then?"

"You do that. He always wins, you know," Pearl contended. "When it comes to cowboys, ain't no one better than my Emmett. Finest man you'd ever want to meet."

Avery sent Shae a sympathetic glance. "Well, you're right about that, Mom," she assured her. "Now I guess it's time for me to show my friend her room down the hall. I'll be staying here with you for the weekend so June can have a few extra days off." She gave a her mother a sweet smile. "It's not often I get to spend time with my mom during rodeo season."

Shae registered the information with surprise. "You sure?" she lip synched carefully so Pearl wouldn't see.

Avery nodded in resigned fashion, as if it were hardly the first time she'd stayed with her mother. "I'll be back a bit later, Mom, okay? We're going to get our bags from the car and then head into the restaurant for a while. Believe me, Shae, you're in for a treat. Nell Granger owns this place, and her steak platter is famous in these parts. Plus, there's usually a poker game on Fridays." She grinned. "Who knows, if you play the part of Lady Luck well enough, you might lasso a cowboy or two before nightfall."

Avery paused for a moment to scan the dozens of old photos of her father on the walls, carefully preserved for posterity. To Shae's surprise, a marked tenderness surfaced in Avery's gaze that she'd never quite witnessed before, tinged with a sense of loss and something more…something akin to…hurt. Burning in Avery's soft brown eyes was a deep pain that still appeared raw after all these years.

"Just be careful what you wish for," Avery whispered in a rocky tone to Shae as she made strides for the door. She turned the knob and gave her mother and June a wave before disappearing down the hall.

6

By the time the two women settled into a cowhide booth in the Golden Wagon Restaurant, like clockwork, a group of cowboys had begun to assemble at a round table in the back of the room by the river rock fireplace. They joked warmly with one another and ribbed a man in a black hat to hurry up and open a sealed deck of cards.

"Sweet Jesus!" whispered Shae, clutching her chest as if she were about to faint. "Did you see those guys over there ready to play poker? They're gorgeous! How could you keep the secret of this town's cowboys away from me for so long?"

Avery rolled her eyes and glanced out the window at the sunset that left a warm glow over the western storefronts and boardwalks of her hometown. "Well, this is where they grow, 'em," she told Shae, unraveling the red-bandana napkin from her silverware and placing it on her lap. She slid a gaze at the collection of rugged men in the corner with the cynical eye of a professional who only considered the best of the best for *My Forever Cowboy*.

Yet nothing prepared Avery for the devastatingly handsome cowboy seated at the table in a black hat, unwrapping the cellophane from a brand new deck of cards. To her astonishment, unwelcome tingles skittered up her back. Handsome men were her stock in trade, but this man had the most stunning blue eyes she'd ever seen, the luminous turquoise of an alpine lake in sunlight, with a depth to his gaze that bowled her over. Goosebumps danced on Avery's skin, despite the fact that she *never* mixed business with pleasure, and she'd steeled herself from the charms of any cowboy for miles for as long as she could remember. It didn't help matters that the man's dark hair and mustache, with the gritty stubble of a growing beard, perfectly offset his high cheekbones, firm chin, and chiseled jawline. But what really seized her curiosity was the peculiar tattoo on the inside of his well-muscled forearm.

It was in the shape of a mandala.

Avery knew about mandalas from her friend Luna who ran a yoga studio in Colorado Springs and often had her students meditate on the symbol. According to Luna, the word meant circle in Sanskrit, and dwelling on mandalas helped her students "embrace inner harmony and wholeness". That sounded like a bunch of New Age gibberish to Avery, yet she was intrigued why a local cowboy, who clearly still had mud caked on his boots and jeans from the day's ranch work, would have such a mysterious tattoo permanently inked on his skin. Though she blinked several times to shake off her odd reaction, his cool demeanor and brooding good looks left her transfixed, in spite of the abrupt appearance of a waitress in a Victorian gown who'd come to take her order.

"Uh, give me the s-steak platter, please," stuttered Avery, rubbing her brows to break her distraction. She made a cursory attempt to scan the others at the corner table, sizing up their features for My Forever Cowboy potential.

"You do know that means *sirloin*, not beef cake, right?" chided the waitress, turning to steal a glance at the men. "My, my, those Iron Feather brothers certainly have caught your eye. If you want, I can introduce you. But be forewarned—some women have cursed me later for the privilege."

"Brothers?" gasped Shae, clutching at the burl-wood table. "Goodness, that's the best looking brood of men I've ever seen!"

"Oh...the Iron Feather brothers," sniffed Avery, recognizing the familiar name. "I was a few years behind them in school, and I heard about how they were sent to the Wilson Ranch for Wayward Boys in their early teens because they tangled with the law."

"*Tangled* is a bit of a stretch," remarked the waitress. "More like waged war against polite society after their folks died in a car crash. The 'brothers' business ain't quite right either. Only three of them are flesh and blood—the two Native American-looking ones and the guy with blonde hair. The other two with blue eyes, they're members of the Hollow family." The waitress nodded at a vintage photo of outlaws in a wood frame decorated with barbed wire on the restaurant wall. "All five of the men at that back table are descendants of the leaders of the Bandits Hollow Gang—Iron Feather and Virgil Hollow.

31

Since their ancestors were as thick as thieves, they consider each other brothers to this day."

Shae's gaze met Avery's. "More facts to memorize for the tourists around here? Dang," she gushed, "that outlaw vibe sure does look good on those cowboys!"

"You having the steak platter too, hon?" the waitress prodded Shae. "Or should I just bring the spyglass from the antiques case in the lobby so you can get a closer look at them?"

"Steak and spyglass sound perfect to me!" giggled Shae. "While you're at it, bring plenty of dessert so I have a reason to stick around and enjoy the eye candy."

"Eye candy?" The waitress arched a brow. "Well, you can call them that till the cows come home. But most folks 'round here call 'em Hell in Black Hats, just like their ancestors."

"I don't mind a little hell raisin'," smiled Shae, "as long as it's sprinkled with fun." She openly gawked at the two dark-haired men with Native-American features, one of which had long hair that fell down his back. Then she switched her focus to the blonde brother who was equally handsome, with a square jaw and sinister look in his eye, before settling on the man with the black hat whose blue eyes could melt the hearts of even the frostiest women.

Including Avery.

Shae spotted the way she whisked her gaze to the floor rather than be caught swiping another peek at him. His was a face of granite, yet with eyes of such pure, vivid blue they could almost see through you…

Shae's eyebrows drew together as the waitress finished scribbling on her notepad and departed with their order. "Can the Iron Feather brothers really be all that bad?" she whispered, glancing down at her bright-pink rodeo shirt and black miniskirt that hugged her body like saran wrap. A mischievous look surfaced in her eyes. "I didn't exactly dress like this to *behave* in Bandits Hollow."

"Stealing cars, rustling cattle, shooting at case workers—those are just some of the rumors I used to hear before they were sent off to reform school. Along with folks mysteriously disappearing who dared to cross any of them. Luckily, most of them resurfaced." Avery shook her head. "But that was when they were teens after their parents died and they ran like a pack of wolves, trying to take care of each other at a remote, ramshackle homestead before the law caught up with them. The local paper claimed they were content to live in the pioneer way, without electricity or running water. They managed to pull it off for nearly a year."

"So they're mavericks!" piped up Shae. "Full of guts and glory, like John Wayne. Doesn't that make them perfect for MFC? Maybe they'll let us take their pictures at the rodeo tomorrow." She tossed her bandana napkin on the table. "Wouldn't hurt to go over to their table and ask—"

Shae got up to leave the booth, when Avery seized her arm. Her tight grip made Shae wince.

"Ouch! What's gotten into you?" Shae scolded, sitting back down and rubbing her skin. She glared at Avery for a moment. "We are here for *work*, you know." Her glossy pink lips curled into a smile. "With maybe just a little hell raisin' on the side."

"They're the wrong kind of *hell*, Shae," Avery insisted in a low tone. "Didn't you hear the waitress? Juvenile records aside, I've lost count of all the girlfriends I've known who got their hearts broken by this or that Iron Feather brother after high school. Apparently they never open up, like their souls are kept under lock and key. And talk about Alpha—they look down on any kind of work that doesn't involve risking their lives riding bulls, racing cars, or fighting in professional arenas. They're as tough as they come, with iron hearts to boot."

"And that's a drawback?" countered Shae. "All I'm after is a good time! Unless you're trying to tell me they'll laugh in my face if I propose a photo opportunity, even though we pay well?"

"Bingo," Avery nodded impatiently. She dared to throw another glance at the back table, noting that the Iron Feather brothers appeared absorbed by their poker game and oblivious to anyone else in the room. "Why, oh why, do they have to be *so* good looking," she sighed, "in that old school, I-can-build-a-ranch-and-hunt-meat-for-your-supper kind of way? Dixie at Stampede would flip if she saw photos of them. She'd probably sell a million copies of our calendar if an Iron Feather brother was in it. But with their reputation, I can't imagine any of them going for it."

Avery's eyes narrowed at the poker game on the back table for a moment, as though calculating in her head the card numbers and patterns of clubs, diamonds, hearts, and spades. "Unless…"

She dropped her gaze to her tailored ivory suit, which she wore like professional armor, her fingers unconsciously pressing out a few wrinkles. Though the waitress came by and set their steak platters on the table, Avery brooded, remaining lost in thought.

"Dig in!" urged Shae, chewing a mouthful of baked

potato. She sliced off a hunk of steak and stuffed it in greedily. "Wow, you were right—the food here is fantastic."

Avery managed to grab a few bites of baked potato, all the while still checking out the Iron Feather brothers' poker game between chews.

"What?" Shae finally broke in. "What is it? If you think those guys are such a bust for MFC, why do you keep peeking at that table?" A glint came to her eyes. "Do you have a crush on one of them? I saw you checking out the guy in the black hat."

"No!" Avery defended, a rush of goosebumps sliding down her neck. She speared a hunk of steak and returned her gaze squarely on her plate. "It's just that a photo of one of them would be like…printing money…wouldn't it? They're better looking than any professional models, and as far as cowboys go, they're the real deal." Her eyes met her assistant's. "We could make a fortune, Shae. As long as we could coax one of them to actually look sincere."

"But if they're so rough and tumble, how would we manage to hogtie an Iron Feather brother into doing it?" Shae spotted an old rifle over the mantle above the river rock fireplace. "Threaten his life?"

"Or his pride," replied Avery. A wicked look arose in her eyes, startling Shae. "I know this might come as a surprise, but I used to play poker after my shift here at the Golden Wagon Restaurant when I was in my teens. I had to do something to supplement my income to take care of my mom—there weren't a lot of options for sixteen-year-olds."

"*You* were a card shark?" Shae gasped in amazement. "Avery Smart has a secret renegade side? No wonder you're a good business woman!" She forked another helping of baked potato into her mouth. "But how does that get us any photos?"

"Simple—blackmail," Avery confided. She slipped off her ivory blazer and carefully folded it on the booth cushion. Then she strategically unbuttoned her cream blouse to reveal more cleavage, pushing up her breasts with her palms to achieve swollen prominence. Pulling off the band from her sleek ponytail, she shook her head, releasing a thick mane of copper hair that cascaded to her shoulders, revealing naturally highlighted strands that shone like spun gold. The way her hair perfectly framed her porcelain features made Shae's breath hitch.

"Whoa," gushed Shae, "you look...awesome, boss! But blackmail? I don't get it." She appeared befuddled. "Do you have some kind of dirt on the Iron Feather brothers that nobody else knows about?"

"Nope," answered Avery. She shot a cocky look at the back table and returned her gaze to Shae. "But the *cards* do."

7

"Hey fellas!" Avery called out, sashaying her hips as she took bold strides toward the poker table across the room. She brazenly pulled up a chair and crossed her long, slim legs, leaning forward so they could catch sight of her cleavage. "You know, I watch *Poker Challenge* on the Vegas Dice Network all the time," she mentioned in an artfully ditzy tone. Her eyes took on a puzzled look. "But try as I might, I can never quite grasp the game. Think you can teach a gal how to play so I can enjoy Vegas someday? I'm Avery, by the way," she said, turning to her assistant. "And this is my friend Shae. Bring over a chair, honey! While you're at it, order us some banana cream pie."

The men around the table fell dead quiet. Aside from the screech of chair legs as Shae dragged a captain's chair across the wood floor, Avery could have heard a pin drop.

"Aw, are you the strong and silent types?" she purred sweetly. "Tell you what, I'll chip in the first fifty bucks for your trouble if you fellas deal me a hand and let me play a round. Maybe I can learn by trying?" She dug into her purse and tossed a fifty-dollar bill onto the table.

"That would be highway robbery, ma'am," stated the man in the black hat, his turquoise-blue eyes sizing her up and finding her wanting.

"A slaughter," added another man at the table.

"Downright road kill," chimed in the man sitting next to him.

Shae was stunned to see Avery summon a fake blush of modesty.

"You don't think I have a prayer?" Avery fanned her face. "All my life I've wanted to play poker, just like in the western movies. It would be a dream come true if you'd give me a short lesson. One little bitty round?"

"Do you even know what Texas Hold 'Em means?" asked the man in the black hat, squinting at her like a badger. Avery was impressed that his eyes actually met hers, rather than drifting to her cleavage. Yet her stomach continued to do flip flops over those incredible blue eyes he trained on her, making her fidget.

"Excuse me," she asked politely, fluttering her lashes to avoid his glare, "who am I addressing?" She was forced to drop her gaze to the table because his soulful eyes seemed like they could see straight into her heart, and she feared detection.

"Grant Hollow," he replied brusquely, tipping his hat. "We're not in the habit of taking advantage of novice players around here, ma'am," he pointed out. "We're the Iron Feather brothers, and we abide by a code of honor. Always."

"Well, think of it as a *teaching session* then," Avery suggested without missing a beat. "It can't be all that hard, right? I assume Texas Hold 'Em means you hang onto your cards till the end, and the rest of the game is dumb luck?"

"In a manner of speaking," Grant replied, his eyes narrowing. "But like anything, experience has a way of improving your luck—"

A tinny rendition of the *Bonanza* theme song interrupted Grant, coming from the blonde man's pocket. He pulled out a cell phone and stared at a text, checking the time and nodding his head. "Look, I gotta get back to the ranch within the hour," he insisted. "If one game is all we got time for, let's get a move on. And if you're gonna play, lady, then for God's sake play. It ain't my problem if you get fleeced."

Quickly, the blonde man seized the cards from Grant and began to deal everyone in—including Avery. "Fifty bucks ante is what the lady started us off with, so chip in, gentlemen."

The other men around the table rolled their eyes, barely tolerating Avery's presence as bills were slapped on the table.

"Oh, one other thing," Avery cut in with the sparkly hope of a first-timer. "If I win, I get to take a picture of the last man in at the Outlaw Days Rodeo tomorrow, okay? My momma would *love* to have a photo of a real-life cowboy. It would make her day."

"Whatever," mumbled the blonde dealer, scanning the men's faces. "You okay with that guys?" After a few nods and shrugs, he finished dealing out two cards to each person.

"All right," the blonde man instructed, "you get to hold two cards in your hand, ma'am, and place a bet or fold."

Shae leaned over and squinted at Avery's hand of two sevens with genuine confusion in her eyes. Her attention was short-lived, however, when the waitress brought over a couple of pieces of pie and set them on a nearby table. Shae scurried to snag a fork and thrust a chunk of the banana cream into her mouth, enjoying the burst of sweetness while the men examined their cards.

"Um, I suppose I can put in another fifty?" Avery mentioned uneasily. She fished in her purse for more bills and placed her bet on the table.

The other players coolly followed suit. Then the blonde dealer set out three more cards. "This here is the flop," he said. "We have the ten of spades, king of diamonds, and seven of spades. After the players bet again, I'll put two more cards down, and you can make any combo from the table and your hand you want. Pairs, a set, a flush, a full house—you get the idea."

This time Grant raised one hundred dollars.

A few moments later, all the men shook their heads and folded their hands. Grant arched a brow as if his gaze could slice through to Avery's soul. No matter how much she tried to steel herself, the extraordinary blue of his eyes made her squirm self-consciously.

"Okay, looks like we're down to two players already," stated the blonde dealer. "You sure you're still in, ma'am? Grant here ain't exactly a stranger to poker."

"Uh, I guess so," Avery said with deliberate uncertainty. She shot a feigned nervous look at Shae, who was too distracted by pie to notice. Avery pulled more bills from her purse and plopped one hundred dollars on the table.

The blonde man dealt another card—the three of clubs.

Avery's eyes flared. "Ooh, do I get to bet on that one, too?" she asked excitedly. She tossed in another fifty.

Grant sighed as though all he wanted was for this infernal game to be over. He slapped his last fifty dollars in the middle.

"He's all in after the turn, ma'am," advised the blonde man. "Which means once I put down the river card, this game's done. You're certain you wanna keep going?"

"Sure!" Avery said with the giddiness of a sixth grader. "I'm having so much fun—I can't believe I'm finally playing poker for reals!"

The blonde man placed the final card on the table—a king of clubs.

"This is the part where you lay down your hand, ma'am," said the blonde man.

Avery watched as Grant set out his cards, revealing the ace and king of hearts. Along with the two kings on the table, it made a whopping three of a kind. Rather than appear smug, his eyes settled with genuine concern on Avery, sending a whole new rush of tingles down her back. She'd never seen a player who wasn't full of himself after her ditzy card-player routine, reveling in his big fat ego before she turned the tables and took him for all he was worth. Nevertheless, this was business—and Avery desperately needed that photo.

"Oh dang," she pouted, her shoulders drooping. "Guess I'm out a few hundred bucks. But thanks for dealing me in," she chirped brightly. "I can't wait to brag about playing poker to my friends! Here goes nothing." Biting her lip, Avery slowly laid out her cards with a wince.

There were two sevens. Combined with the seven and two

kings on the table, her hand made the blonde dealer's mouth drop. He blinked a few times, just to make certain.

"Ma'am," he said, swallowing carefully, "you've got a full house."

"A what?" Avery nodded, looking around the room. "It is kind of crowded in here, huh?"

"No, I mean your cards," he said. "A full house beats three of a kind. You...won."

"Don't spend it all in one place!" remarked the Native American-looking man with long hair. He slapped Grant on the back and laughed. "Looks like you're out a wad of cash, bro. And a cheesy tourist photo to boot. Guess you'll be trying to win money at the rodeo tomorrow, huh? No break from bull riding for you."

"Does this mean I get to keep the money?" asked Avery in a timid voice. "With an I.O.U. for a photo?" She glanced up expectantly at Grant, relishing the shock in his eyes as he squared his shoulders as though prepping himself for the photo prospect. He nodded slowly. Avery began counting her money at the table with glee like a total amateur, but her attention was shattered by a booming voice that cut through the restaurant.

"Well I'll be damned. Is that Avery Smart? Emmett Smart's daughter?"

A rancher who'd walked into the room with his wife and children made a beeline for Avery. "I didn't think this town was good enough for you to darken the Golden Wagon Restaurant anymore, with your fancy photography business and all."

Startled, Avery glanced up, only to see Grant's thick

eyebrows bearing down and his cool, blue eyes boring into hers. In that moment, his expression registered that he knew he'd been played—and he wasn't happy about it.

"*You're* Emmett Smart's daughter?" Grant said. "The three-time, all-around cowboy at the Outlaw Days Rodeo? The same guy who was renowned for winning at poker in this town?"

"Hey Randy," Avery swiftly changed the subject and turned around in her chair to face the rancher. To her surprise, Randy wasn't at all the strapping boy she recalled from high school whose bulls won best of show at the county fair. He'd grown a big belly and an even bigger attitude, and she was grateful she'd had the good sense not to marry his kind after graduation. Unlike the rest of her girlfriends, who'd thrown themselves at a myriad of cowboys who took them for granted till their hearts were all shriveled up. Avery caught his wife's eyes—it was Darla, one of her former classmates. Predictably, she appeared tired and beaten down, with three young children hanging onto her and screaming for ice cream. One of her little girls threw herself onto the floor and pounded her fists. Her mother simply stared at the floor.

Avery remembered her as a talented teen who'd wanted to be a photographer once, like herself. Darla had even won a 4-H competition with her evocative photos of the historic architecture of Bandits Hollow, yet she was barely recognizable now. She was forty pounds heavier with bags under her eyes, the kind that looked like they'd need a whole lot more than a good night's sleep to cure.

"I'm just in town for a little while," mentioned Avery in a dismissive tone to Randy, casting a quick glance at Shae, who

43

was diving into her second piece of pie. With a sigh, Avery took compassion on Darla and picked up her little girl from the floor, setting her to her feet. "Nice to see you, Darla," she smiled kindly. "Hope you try the pie here." She looked longingly at the piece that Shae had already half-devoured. "It's really good."

"You don't fool me," Randy said with a cocky smile. "You're here to check on your crazy mama, huh? Does she still drool in her coffee? I've spotted her here in the restaurant a few times, acting like your dad is still alive and waiting for him. Folks say she's batty from living in haunted room number thirteen."

He leaned in close and ran his hand suggestively down Avery's back, lingering at her waist. A rush of revulsion turned Avery's stomach—she knew he'd had a crush on her in high school, and she'd tried to rebuff him then, too. Though she wanted to deck him now, she simply attempted to move a step back, but he held her closer and leaned into her ear. "Too bad you ain't got nobody to help take care of your crackpot mama," he said. "Guess that's what you get for running off to the big city and acting like you're better than everybody. But if you ever need a *real* man to remind you of hometown warmth, you just whistle."

When his hand lowered to her ass, all at once, Avery felt like she was in his pickup truck again after the junior dance when he'd tried to strong arm her. She'd delivered a knuckle sandwich that gave him a fat lip that night, but she was in a public place right now and didn't want to mar the reputation of Nell's restaurant. Picking up on the alarm on Avery's face,

Grant instantly stood to his feet. When Randy attempted to cup her butt cheek, he headed straight for him.

"Time to move along, mister," Grant said in a deep tone. The fire in his blue eyes warned Randy not to mess with him. "This ain't how you treat women in Nell's restaurant. Or anywhere else, for that matter."

"Who's this," Randy said to Avery, "your new boyfriend or something?"

"Nope," replied Grant before she could answer. "Just another player at a poker table alongside a mighty sharp lady. She won the game fair and square."

At the sight of Grant's large, balled fists, making ripples of muscles dance up his thick arms, Randy removed his hand from Avery with a sullen look. "Well don't believe the slick clothes she's wearing," he scoffed. "She's from the same ranch dirt as you and me, pal. Bet you wanted to keep that a secret too, now didn't you, Avery?"

"Nothing about my life's a secret, Randy," Avery snapped. "As a matter of fact, I *do* take care of my mother. I pay all her room and board here, along with professional nursing care, because it's the right thing to do. And I don't hide that from anybody."

At that moment, Avery's eyes grew twice their size when she saw her mother silently slip into the restaurant. She sat down in a cowhide booth, holding up the photo of her father, as quiet as a shadow. But when she turned her head and spotted Grant Hollow, her face blanched. Pearl blinked several times and gazed at the photo, then back at Grant, like she'd seen a ghost.

"It's him!" Pearl shrieked, her voice ringing through the

restaurant. She pointed at Grant. "Oh, Emmett," she tapped insistently on the photo as though waking her husband from a deep sleep, "it's really him! The one who can take me to you, I swear! He knows where you are!"

Avery's cheeks flashed beet red. Before she could stop her, Pearl got up from her booth and shuffled quickly over to Grant, grabbing onto his arm like a life line. "You'll help us, right?" she begged, tugging repeatedly on his sleeve. Then she gave him a soft smile and reached up to stroke his cheek. "I knew it wasn't a dream. All along, I knew you were real. I just knew it."

8

Pearl accidentally dropped her photo of her late husband on the floor. "Oh mercy!" she cried, fumbling to pick it up. She carefully smoothed out the paper with her fingers. "I'm so sorry, Emmett—please forgive me." She glanced up at Grant with imploring eyes. "You remember me, don't you? It was in the winter, ten years ago—we met out in the woods behind the Lazy C Ranch. I was collecting pine boughs for Christmas, and I got turned around…"

As her words trailed off, Grant gently wrapped an arm around Pearl's fragile frame. He gazed into her eyes with a look of such penetrating kindness that it struck Avery's heart, despite her shock over her mother's outburst. Confused, she began to wonder if all those tall tales about the Iron Feather brothers' cold hearts were really true.

"Why don't we step over to those comfy armchairs in the

lobby? We could talk about old times," Grant assured Pearl in a warm tone. "You up for that?"

Clutching her precious photo to her chest, Pearl nodded. Grant carefully escorted her out of the restaurant and away from the prying eyes of strangers.

Avery stood in her tracks, dumbfounded. She quickly gathered her senses and made swift strides to catch up with them, when she felt a tug on her arm. It was June.

"I'm so sorry!" she burst with creases of worry on her forehead. "I just went to the restroom for a minute, and Pearl disappeared on me—"

"It-It's okay," Avery replied, her eyes glued in amazement at the way Grant and Pearl were seated in the lobby with such ease. They smiled and chatted like they'd known each other for ages. "Feel free to take a long weekend off and I'll see you Tuesday morning, all right?"

"Sure, thank you!" June replied. "See you next week," she said with a wave before heading back up the stairs.

Avery tiptoed toward Grant and Pearl in the lobby, cautious about disrupting their warm repartee. What intrigued her most was the calm, easy banter they seemed to enjoy—it had been forever since she'd seen her mother so relaxed. Avery managed to slip into an armchair beside Pearl without disturbing their conversation, remaining as quiet as a mouse.

"I tell ya," Pearl told Grant, "It's been good for my soul to talk about the old days in Bandits Hollow. I had no idea you'd known Emmett since you were little."

"If it weren't for him, ma'am," Grant affirmed, "I never would have gone into rodeo. He used to hang out with kids in the side corrals after his events, generously showing us all the tips he knew. We really looked up to him." He gave Pearl a sincere smile that made his gorgeous blue eyes shine all the more. "Especially since he was the three-time, all-around cowboy in our town." He slanted a gaze at Avery beside her mother. "Of course, he was renowned for beating *everyone* in Bandits Hollow at poker, too."

Avery's cheeks prickled with heat, and she ducked her eyes. There was no doubt in her mind he was on to her now.

"Thank you for taking the time to visit with me," Pearl patted Grant's hand. "I apologize, but I must retire to my room—I get tired easily these days. You'll come see me again, won't you?"

"You bet," Grant replied kindly. He watched with concern as Pearl got up and slowly shuffled up the grand staircase to the second floor. As soon as she disappeared, Avery cleared her throat.

"I-I don't know how to thank you, Mr. Hollow," she said on the verge of tears, overcome by his generosity. "My mother, she um, gets…confused…sometimes." Avery swallowed a deep breath and blinked back her emotions. "You had a such calming affect on her."

Grant tipped his hat. "She's just scared, ma'am."

"What?"

"I'd be willing to bet," he folded his thick arms thoughtfully, "that she's seen something most folks don't."

Avery stared at him, puzzled.

"Happens all the time. A horse you're working with reacts to something you don't notice. Later on, you accidentally discover what it was and realize everything was real. Innocent creatures are like that—they don't have a reason to lie."

49

"I-I know you heard they way Randy talked. You know, about my mother being...crazy," Avery confessed carefully. She glanced into the restaurant, relieved to find that he and his family were distracted by their meal. "A-Are you trying to say my Mom's room upstairs really *is* haunted?"

"No. I'm saying *she* is. Maybe, if you tried looking at things her way, you might understand where she's coming from."

"I don't understand *anything*," Avery said, choking down a frustration in her throat that had been building for over a decade. "A psychiatrist once tested her and told me she's not schizophrenic or delusional, so there's nothing he can do with medication. He said my mom simply made up a story to deal with the trauma of my dad's sudden death, which she clings to for survival." Avery hugged her waist, staring at the floor for a moment. "She thinks she saw some ghost or angel ten years ago who told her my dad isn't gone and is waiting for her. To be honest, I go along with it. I don't have the heart to take her hope away."

Avery sighed and eyed the grand staircase as though searching for the invisible trail of her mother's footsteps. She shook her head and turned to Grant. "You know, I can't help wondering why you two had such an easy rapport. Have you ever met her before?"

"No, ma'am. Only your father Emmett," Grant said. His lips curled into a wry smile. "Who, by the way, used to beat my dad and everyone else in this town regularly at the rodeo. *And at Texas Hold 'Em.*"

Avery glanced away, attempting to hide her racing pulse.

"Look, no matter what things may seem like," she nodded her head toward the restaurant, "It's not like I was counting cards or cheating. I won by following the rules. But the way you helped my mom just now—I don't feel right about taking your money or making you feel obligated for a photo. It's literally been years since I've seen my mom so happy, having an actual conversation with someone."

Grant stood up and gave Avery a big, warm smile that blew her away. It was the kind of smile that was more than charming—it revealed he understood her pain, maybe even wished he could soothe it a little, because he knew what it was like to live in a world of hurt.

"Well, ma'am, I appreciate the offer," he said, "but I *never* renege on my bets. Besides, I can't afford to earn the wrong reputation at that poker table," he shot a glance at the Iron Feather brothers still playing cards, "much less live it down with those slackers. I'll be at the rodeo tomorrow. So you best use your camera quick, in case the bull wins."

"The bull?" Avery looked at him quizzically.

"I'll be bull riding, ma'am. Ain't that the whole point of going to a rodeo? But I will ask you one thing."

Avery held her breath, waiting.

"Don't ever lie to me again, Miss Smart."

He glared at her with enough ice in his gaze to make her breath stop in her throat. Then he flashed another mega-watt smile that sent far too many tingles into places where the sun didn't shine, causing Avery to squirm in her chair. "Or I'm coming after my money you swindled by pretending to be… easy." He gave her a wink, his eyes tracing her cleavage and lingering with admiration on the curves of her breasts and hips. "With interest."

9

"Avery! Avery! Did you see this, boss?"

Squinting through the rodeo dust, Avery spied Shae sprinting toward her in a pink, polka-dotted halter top and cut-off jean shorts with pink cowboy boots, making her appear more like a pole dancer than a professional assistant. She waved a magazine in her hand, her blonde curls bouncing and her smile a mile wide. When she reached Avery, she grabbed her arm and shoved a glossy picture of a cowboy in her face. For a moment, Avery feared Shae had gone off-kilter, obsessing about a cowboy's photo like her mother.

"They had a stack of these magazines by the concession stand, free for rodeo ticket holders!" Shae jumped up and down excitedly. "Do you have *any* idea who this man is?"

Avery rubbed the gritty dust from her eyes. When she took the magazine, she couldn't tell who the man on the cover was, riding a bull in a swirl of dirt.

"That's Grant Hollow. The same guy you beat at poker last night!"

"Uh, okay," Avery replied, a bit confused.

Shae flapped her hands with giddy enthusiasm. "He was the Bull Riding World Champion last year, and the year before that. Avery—he's *famous!*" She grabbed the magazine and flipped through the pages until she came to an article, holding it up. It was a profile of Grant Hollow on his winning streak. "Can you believe our luck? He's still going to do a photo, right? This calendar's gonna be a bestseller!"

"Now, now," Avery felt a warm breath against her ear, "it ain't polite to talk about people behind their backs."

Avery whipped around, her heart racing. It was Grant, grinning at her with a mischievous look in those ridiculously beautiful eyes. He tipped his hat.

"Good morning, ladies. I don't normally authorize photos, especially for commercial *calendars*." He glared at the two women. "But I'm not the kind of man who goes back on his word." He turned to Avery, glancing at the professional camera around her neck. "So you get one shot, ma'am. Kind of like bull riding. You have eight seconds while I'm on that bull to take my picture, then we're done. Because real cowboys *don't pose*."

"Deal!" cried Shae, reaching out to vigorously shake his hand. She yanked a folded piece of paper and a pen from the back pocket of her cut-offs and thrust them into Grant's palms. "It'll just take a second for you to fill out this release form," she insisted. "Don't forget your phone number," she smiled.

Grant unfolded the form and brooded for a moment over

the contents. To Avery's surprise, he stepped behind her and boldly used her back as a writing surface, smoothing the paper over her red blouse and letting his hand linger for a few seconds at the curve of her waist. "My Forever Cowboy—is that the name of your business, Miss Smart?" he remarked in a low tone that she found unbearably sexy. "So you're going to make money off me *again*?"

He leaned in so close this time she could feel his breath against her neck, sending goosebumps across her skin. "This never had anything to do with your mother's sad story, did it? What a pretty liar you are."

Avery gasped, waging a war inside between the embarrassment she felt and a crazy desire to spin around and kiss him. Never before had she found a cowboy so irresistible. It took all her strength to straighten her shoulders and coolly swivel when she felt he was done writing. She held her head high and faced him. One thing she knew how to do was to become the Ice Queen when she needed it.

"Everything goes to my mother," she stated flatly, "and that's the truth. You saw her. She's only forty-six and she behaves like a disoriented old woman, even though doctors say she doesn't have dementia. It's like she's been under a…spell… all this time. And it takes a hefty sum to keep her in round-the-clock care, because I refuse to put her in a home. When my dad died, we were flat broke. And for your informations, Mr. Hollow, My Forever Cowboy is the cash cow that keeps her care going." Avery dropped her gaze and stared at the ground, her voice becoming fragile. "In case it ever turns out that *I'm not here forever.*"

Grant lifted her chin with his finger and stared straight into her eyes. His attention seemed uncommonly compassionate, and for the life of her, Avery wanted to fall into those big blue eyes and drown in the comfort they promised. But then Grant lips broke into a smile, making his eyes twinkle.

"Maybe all she needs is to have a little fun," he said, his gaze filled with challenge like he harbored a secret.

"Up next is our own hometown hero, Grant Hollow!" bellowed the announcer from the rodeo grandstand, breaking off their conversation. "Two-time World Champion! We've got a very special Charbray bull with his number on it, the notorious Steel Phantom. Put your hands together to cheer him on, folks. And Grant, wherever you are, get your rear end to the chute, pronto!"

The crowds in the bleachers of the Outlaw Days Rodeo thundered their applause in admiration. Grant slung his thumbs into his Wrangler jeans front pockets and gave Avery an easy smile. "Better hurry, Miss Smart—my number's up to ride. See you in eight seconds."

10

Nerves snapped and sizzled through Grant's limbs as his heartbeat began to climb. He mounted the bull in the chute, feeling the animal's muscles writhe beneath him in electric anticipation. This challenge, even at regional rodeos like Outlaw Days, never grew stale. If it did, that's how a cowboy ended up dead. Champion one week, broken in two the next. Those were the odds Grant faced every time he climbed onto a bull—the high-octane stakes of his life.

Just like Virgil Hollow and Iron Feather, he thought, when they led the Bandits Hollow Gang. Despite all their preparation, holding up stagecoaches and trains always came down to a precious few seconds. A time out of time, where everything seemed to slow, almost like a portal to another dimension. Grant knew that zone like the back of his hand— one of power and focus that some said he was addicted to, where all sound and distraction disappeared. For onlookers, his rides were an explosion of spins, thrusts, spirals, and plunges with dust erupting like land mines from beneath the bull's hooves. But for Grant, those moments were where he and the bull became one, dancing in air—

Eight seconds of eternity...

Drawing a deep breath, he grabbed the rope over the bull's withers and ran his fist up and down to warm the rosin, making the fibers stick to his glove. Then he slid a glance at the indigo tattoo on his forearm of a large wheel made of interlocking circles.

"Balance, unity, eternity," he whispered, exactly the way Emmett Smart had taught him as a boy. It was Emmett's secret code, one he'd learned from his Ute friend who was an expert horseman, a reminder to think of nothing but moving with the animal like an extension of its spine until you hit the mysterious zone. That's when your spirits felt like one—and you could ride forever. Emmett used to coach the local kids on steers after school, spinning his lariat in endless circles while he described the nuances of the sport he loved. He told them of the power of roundness, inherent in the Native American wisdom of medicine wheels, dream catchers, circle dances and sun discs marked by the four directions. Viewing the ride as a circle, what some called a mandala, was the key, Emmett said, to staying on a bull or a bronc. Rather than fight the animal in a typical man-against-nature battle, he showed them the power of balance and how to become one with it. Then the eight seconds would no longer be a struggle. Instead, it was a glimpse into...

Eternity.

Grant inserted his glove into the crescent handle of the

rope and ran the tail end as tight as hell around his hand. Feeling confident, he nodded to the gate man to indicate it was time for lift off.

The cowboy threw open the chute, and as Grant expected, the blue-gray bull Steel Phantom, bred by Lander Iron Feather, vaulted in air like he'd been shot from a launching pad. The young bull that was already climbing up the ranks on the rodeo circuit and renowned for his wild dips and spins soared in the air like a rocket.

The crowds in the bleachers stood to their feet with a roar. Steel Phantom was a star, his hooves barreling to the ground like a jackhammer, aloft again in seconds with moves that defied gravity. Before Grant could even catch his breath from the first plunge, they were already soaring once again into the sky.

Flying.

With his notorious feats of agility, Steel Phantom swung his hips to the left at the beginning of his buck and then whipped them to the right in mid-air to produce a mind-boggling spin. His moves seemed physically impossible, given his nearly one-ton weight, yet he kept barreling into airborne spirals as if he could reach the stars. Each time he switched directions on a dime, Grant remained steady as if his seat were fused to the animal's back, still hearing Emmett's words echoing in his brain. Unity, balance, eternity. No matter how hard the bull pitched and bucked, crashing his hooves to the ground, Grant stayed centered. Steel Phantom had yet to be ridden for eight seconds in a recognized rodeo—and Grant fully intended to be the first.

He was so absorbed in the ride that he didn't notice Avery

snapping pictures from behind the safety of a barrel a few yards outside the bucking zone. It was the "suicide barrel", a station that required a liability release form signed by photographers to use for the purpose of catching the very best shots. Despite the dirt and dust distributed by Steel Phantom's furious hooves, she snapped her shutter faster than a ticker tape, catching Grant from every possible angle. Avery didn't normally do action shots, but she couldn't deny that any photograph of a cowboy as authentic as Grant Hollow would be like winning the commercial calendar lottery.

When the buzzer rang, the crowds filled the stands with their victory cheers.

"We have a landmark here today!" the announcer cried. "Grant Hollow is the first bull rider *ever* to clear eight seconds on Steel Phantom. What a feat, folks! It doesn't surprise us that one of Bandits Hollow's own managed to show Steel Phantom who's boss."

As the announcer kept talking, Grant scrambled away from the bull until he was several yards clear of his horns and hooves. He swiveled around and watched Steel Phantom get distracted by a bull fighter in a clown outfit running circles around him, doing his job to keep the bull away from the newly-dismounted rider. At that moment, a big grin surfaced on Grant's face, his eyes glinting in triumph. Just before he threw his black cowboy hat into the crowd to celebrate, Avery trotted closer and snapped his picture

He looked like a million bucks.

Grant's face was aglow from a feat that had never been achieved before, with the kind of genuine cowboy elation that could never be faked.

Even as she took the photo, butterflies leaped in Avery's stomach—she knew it was the best picture she'd ever captured in her life. She took a few more shots for good measure. All at once, she spied a dust devil barreling toward Grant.

In a rage, Steel Phantom had dodged past the bull fighter, a ball of fury, and steamrolled into Grant, lifting him with his horns and vaulting him in air. Another bull fighter swooped in to help drive the bull toward the exit pen, while two wranglers on horseback charged toward Steel Phantom to help convince him. All the while, Avery dashed to Grant's side.

But Grant didn't see any of that.

All he saw was black.

11

In the darkness, pinpricks of light began to emerge.

Grant blinked, feeling numb over his entire body, except for a sore spot that ached on his ribs. He rubbed his side for a moment and sat up on his elbows to gaze at the distant stars. As his eyes adjusted, he saw a dark silhouette move silently in front of him, its contours highlighted by the moon.

An owl called, its lonesome sound ringing through the night.

The figure turned in the direction of the call. Grant made out the features of a man, and it was like looking into a mirror —he had the same bone structure with a black cowboy hat. For a moment, Grant wondered if he'd died, and perhaps his spirit was staring at himself, at his own broken body, before ascending to become one of the stars. But then the man faced him head on. In the moonlight, Grant could feel the weight of his stare, sending shivers down his spine. There was something old, maybe even ancient in that gaze, as though the man had seen centuries pass and his spirit had grown more faceted from the experience. To Grant's surprise, a great horned owl landed on the man's shoulder, its sharp ear tufts limned by the moonlight. The owl made another call, urgent this time with yellow eyes flared, as if prompting the man.

"Her time's coming," the man said in a low tone of gravel. "Let her go."

Grant had no idea what he was talking about, when he felt something shake his shoulder hard. He blinked and rubbed his eyes, opening them again.

Sunlight stung his vision—

For a moment, all Grant could see was coppery hair with strands of gold highlighted by the sun. He squinted and made out the lovely face of Avery Smart, her brows drawn in concern.

Instantly, she hooked her elbows beneath Grant's arm pits and proceeded to drag his weight with all her might. When Grant realized what was happening, that he was still in the rodeo arena near a two-thousand-pound bull that hadn't been driven to the exit pen yet, he stumbled to his feet and turned the tables on Avery. Scooping her into his large arms, he hugged her close and made a mad dash for the fence.

"Good thing you're light!" he cried, his feet drumming beneath him. A cowboy swung open a nearby gate. Grant rushed through, panting for breath as the cowboy slammed it shut. He held Avery so tightly to his chest, she could feel his heart hammering through his shirt as if he didn't quite believe they'd made it to safety.

"You've heard of *Dances with Wolves?*" said the announcer.

"Looks to me like Grant Hollow was dancing with the photographer! Am I the only who's noticed he hasn't put her down yet? Let's give that cowboy a hand for protecting a lady the old fashioned way."

The crowd applauded and whistled their approval.

"I've never had to clear the arena before I sprinted to the fence before." Grant smiled, his face so close to Avery's he could kiss her. The glint in his eye revealed he'd thought about it.

"Clear the arena? What am I, an empty beer can?" Avery replied, unable to hide the warmth that suffused her cheeks. The truth was, his muscled biceps felt heavenly against her body. And from this vantage point, she got an even closer look at his to die-for eyes.

"I didn't mean it that way." A smile teased Grant's lips, which where perilously close to hers. "A woman like you couldn't be trash if you tried." He paused, his eyes tracing the amber highlights that perfectly framed her beautiful face. "More like striking gold." He took in the warm brown of her eyes and the curve of her mouth, which Avery found sexy to the point of excruciating. "Next time, though," Grant scolded, "I suggest you don't try to rescue one of your photo subjects. Bulls are non-discriminating—they'll take out anybody."

Avery couldn't help noticing his arms squeezed tighter when he said that, as if he were still trying to keep her close and safe. Oh, how she wanted to lean her head back on his broad chest and absorb that wonderful, secure feeling, tucking it inside her heart for hard times. Truth be told, it was a feeling she hadn't known since her father died—that glow in your heart when you know someone loves you so much he'd do anything to keep you from harm. But that was all gone now. Besides, Avery was here in a purely professional capacity—she knew damn well that any feelings of security with cowboys were a mirage.

"I-I don't usually do action shots," she declared. "You were the exception, remember? Because you refused to pose. So you can put me down now, Mr. Hollow."

Grant gazed into her eyes with a devilish amusement that made their vibrant blue flicker like a methane flame. "Do I have to?" His lips slipped into a sly grin. "May I remind you that I don't work for you, Miss Smart? Our photo shoot was a one-time deal," he leaned in to whisper in her ear, "which means I don't have to take orders from you."

Goosebumps fanned over Avery's skin. The tickling warmth of Grant's breath against her ear, along with that husky voice she could listen to all day, was like city-girl catnip that set her body ablaze in places that had no business being ignited in public. Avery sucked in a breath, closing her eyes momentarily to fight the sensation. Then she wriggled hard, elbowing Grant until he slowly set her to her feet, his hand lingering at the small of her back as though he didn't really intend to let go. The gleam in his eyes told her he'd enjoyed every second of her body against his.

Avery dusted off her jeans and pressed out a few crinkles on her red blouse, more to distract herself than to straighten the fabric. "I'll have you know," she asserted, "the only reason I attempted to rescue you was because you looked like you were knocked out for a few seconds and couldn't defend yourself." She set her hands on her hips. "What did you mean, anyway, when you said, 'Her time's coming. Let her go'?"

Grant met her gaze, puzzled.

"That's what you mumbled, while you were laying down in the arena."

He stared off in the distance and shook his head, recalling the odd, dream-like images that had sifted through his thoughts. They made no sense at all.

"I don't know," he replied. The image of the man that looked so much like himself uttering those mysterious words still rattled him, but it wasn't like he had a guidebook to understand it. "Must have been delirious," he shrugged, casting a glance at the concession stand. "Or maybe hungry." He spotted Shae in a line for burgers, dressed in her pink, polka-dot halter top and cut-off shorts with an eager gathering of cowboys milling around and enjoying her perky attention. She was busy writing on a notepad, grinning like she'd won the lottery—or in her case, managed to get half a dozen cowboys' phone numbers. "Sure looks like your assistant is taking advantage of the, um, lunch crowd," Grant remarked.

At that moment, Dusty Watson's vintage red pickup turned into the parking lot with a load of hay, kicking up gravel and dropping sprigs of alfalfa. Avery waved at her former neighbor, who had a few acres near the ranch where she grew up and often helped her dad during calving season. She thought it was odd Dusty was taking time out to go to the rodeo, since he obviously had a load of hay to deliver. But when she shielded her eyes from the sun to gain a closer look, her mouth dropped in shock.

There, in the passenger's side of Dusty's old truck, was her *mother*.

Avery gasped. "What the—"

"If you'll excuse me, Miss Smart," Grant smiled wickedly, "I have a date with a lovely lady to watch the rodeo this afternoon. She told me in the lobby of the Golden Wagon Hotel that she *loves* rodeos."

He gave Avery a casual wave as he proceeded to saunter with long, swinging strides toward the parking lot, his Wrangler jeans hugging his body far too well for Avery's comfort level. When he reached Dusty's passenger side door, he opened it and, to Avery's astonishment, gallantly lifted her mother from the vehicle like a fragile bird, setting her to her feet. Pearl's eyes creased, unaccustomed to being outside in daylight for long. After chatting briefly with Dusty, Grant escorted Pearl toward the rodeo grandstand, helping her watch out for stones and ruts along the trail. Dusty peeled out of the parking lot, losing a bale from the side of his truck, and headed for the highway.

"Oh my God," sputtered Avery, watching as Grant and Pearl climbed up the steps of the grandstand to join two older women who were seated near the top. They wore long, old-fashioned dresses more suited for the pioneer era than the present day, and they grinned at her mother like they were long-lost friends. In no time, the three women were chatting and sharing popcorn while pointing at the most good-looking cowboys competing in the arena. Baffled, Avery tightened her fists.

"What on earth's going on?" she fumed under her breath, feeling violated. "How could anyone remove my mother from the hotel without bothering to ask me?" Shaking her head, she began marching toward the grandstand in a huff.

Climbing over several rows, Avery finally made it to the

upper seats of the grandstand and caught her breath, forced by her lungs to remember Bandits Hollow's elevation of 9,000 feet. She glared at the three seated women who were flanked by Grant.

"How in heaven's name did you get here?" she scolded Pearl. "Who gave you permission to—"

"Is this the high-spirited young gal you were tellin' us about?" Jubilee cut her off, turning to Pearl.

"Ain't she a beauty?" Pearl replied, beaming. "Jubilee and Granny T., this is my daughter Avery. She's a professional photographer, too."

"I declare," remarked Evangeline, squinting at Avery with her timber-wolf eyes that could peer into souls, "she's a right bossy thing, too."

Before Avery could spit out another word, Grant stood up and pointed toward the concession stand.

"Aren't you supposed to be taking more pictures, Miss Smart?" he said. "Your assistant looks like she's getting down to business."

Avery looked closer, only to see Shae handing out her business card to more cowboys. The older women began to giggle.

"My my," Jubilee slapped her thigh, "ain't she got a swarm of bees heading for her honey! What kind of *business* do you actually run, Miss Avery?"

Heat prickled Avery's cheeks at the insinuation. "Commercial *photography*," she insisted squaring her shoulders and lifting her chin in dignity. "That woman down there is my assistant and talent scout. She's doing her job by looking for new prospects."

"Well, she sure is racking and stacking 'em," sniffed Evangeline. "Next thing you know, she'll have 'em hogtied and branded for home delivery."

"Ooh, home delivery? I sure like the cowboy in the green shirt. Can I order that one?" Jubilee squealed. "Look at those broad shoulders and muscled arms—"

"Not if I get to him first!" broke in Pearl. "My bacon cornbread never fails to reel in a cowboy."

"Mother!" Avery snapped. "What's gotten into you—"

Her outburst was interrupted by the sound of a throaty laugh. Avery turned, only to see Grant chuckling at the women's spicy commentary. "Careful, ladies," he warned, staring at Shae and her cowboy cohorts, "it's starting to get racier now. You might have to cover your eyes."

"Nothing doing," giggled Jubilee, pointing at a cowboy who was proudly unbuttoning his shirt for Shae to reveal his six-pack abs. "We've got the hottest seats in the house. This is better than Chippendales."

They watched as Shae pulled out a small bottle from her purse and emptied its contents into her hand. She quickly rubbed oil on the cowboy's chest and instructed him to strip off the rest of his shirt completely. Then she backed up and made a rectangle with her thumbs and forefingers, peering through her makeshift camera lens to judge whether he was My Forever Cowboy material. The smile on her face was confirmation.

"Can I apply for *her* job?" asked Pearl, her eyes glued to the young man's well-developed chest, sending the other women into peals of laughter.

"It's gettin' even better now," reported Evangeline,

nodding at an enterprising cowboy who dashed to a nearby spigot and turned on the water, grabbing the attached hose. He sprayed an unsuspecting cowboy until his shirt was glistening wet and clung to his chest like a second skin, revealing every sculpted muscle. In a heartbeat, the cowboy got him back with a bucket of water from a trough, and a full-fledged water fight ensued. Naturally, the men turned on Shae, splashing her until her curls drooped past her face like drowned poodle, but she didn't care. Shae laughed before rooting around for another bucket to fight back.

"How soon do you think this will turn into mud wrestling?" Evangeline noted, withdrawing a vintage pocket watch from her dress to check the time.

"If I know cowboys, and mind you, I've raised my share," Jubilee replied, "they'll be wallowing like pigs in seconds flat."

A big guffaw erupted, and all of a sudden Avery realized it was her mother laughing. Not just any laugh—a robust sound from deep within her belly that sent crinkles of joy to her eyes. The shaft of sunlight that sliced across her face illuminated her mirth.

Avery sucked air. It had been years since she'd seen her mother like that, looking downright...

Happy.

And she couldn't deny how nice her mother's face appeared in the sun, warming her cheeks to a honeyed hue, compared to the ashy complexion she always had in her hotel room where the shades were permanently drawn. To Avery's surprise, an arm wrapped around her shoulder.

"Wanna join 'em?" Grant said with a gleam in his eyes, nodding at Shae and her cohorts. His gaze roamed down the swells of Avery's breasts and hips. "Something tells me you'd look good with a little mud on you."

"You go first," she sassed back. "Why aren't you down there already, cowboy? Mud slinging seems right up your alley."

Grant smirked at Avery's whip-smart reply. "Well, if you must know, I have to go now. I promised Barrett Iron Feather I'd help him practice heading and healing for his upcoming roping event."

"Chicken," Avery taunted, noticing Shae's wet halter top left little to the imagination, but she couldn't be having a better time. Avery lifted her gaze to the position of the sun overhead. "I should go now, too, and take more photos while the light's still decent—if I can get one of those cowboys to shower in time." She turned to her mother. "I'll give you a ride back to the hotel, Mom, as soon as Shae and I are done."

"Oh, we ain't going back to the hotel," Pearl corrected her. "Jubilee invited us over to the Lazy C Ranch for dinner tonight. Can't wait! Ain't that right, Grant?"

"What? Mom, you haven't left the hotel in ten solid years before this," Avery said, flabbergasted. "It was a stretch for you to even be at the restaurant last night, remember? How are you going to handle dinner with total strangers?"

"They're *not* strangers!" Pearl answered vehemently. She pointed with confidence at Grant. "I told you in the restaurant I met him in the woods ten years ago. Weren't you listening? Jubilee here is his grandma, and this is her friend Granny T. We're going to sit at the Lazy C Ranch and chat about old times in Bandits Hollow." She glared at Avery with a distinct stubbornness in her eyes. "Besides, Jubilee promised me a piece of her thimbleberry pie. Sounds downright heavenly, if you ask me."

Pearl yanked out her photo of her husband and gazed into his eyes. "Don't you think your daughter should take a break from her business, Emmett, and try and be social for a change?"

Avery wanted to crawl inside a hole and die. It always ruffled her feathers when her mother spoke to her father's photo—this time in public, no less. She sighed, slanting a weary gaze at Grant. The traces of a cocky smile on his face made a lightbulb go off in her head.

"This is your way of getting back at me, isn't it?" she accused, folding her arms. "For winning at poker last night and blackmailing you into a photo. Seriously, was it really all that bad?"

The light that danced in Grant's eyes flickered all the more with pleasure at Avery's exasperation. "Your mom looked like she could use a little fresh air," he said, fending her off. "It doesn't hurt to have fun with women closer to her own age for a change. Imagine that."

Avery's eyes narrowed, but when she spotted the excitement on her mother's face, she realized Pearl had already set her heart on dinner with her new-found friends. But how would Grant and his grandmother react if she launched into one of her odd ramblings at their home? Feeling cornered, she tapped her foot and turned to Grant

"You know this means I'm going to have to come with her, right?"

"Be my guest," Grant said with mischievous look, as if that had been his plan all along.

Geez, who snookered who this time? Avery thought with a sigh, marveling at how he'd switched the game on her.

"But no pictures, Miss Smart," Grant continued. "This is my family's heritage homestead—we're not for commercial resale." He leaned in closer so only Avery could hear him. "And just so you know, you won't be the boss at our house."

"Then who is?" Avery shot back.

Grant couldn't help enjoying the feisty look in her eyes. "Why, Grandma Jubilee, of course. Don't worry, I think you're going to like her thimbleberry pie."

12

"And then," said Jubilee said, clutching her tummy in a fit of giggles, "there I was, frozen stiff in front of a cattle stampede like a total idiot! Lord have mercy, I was scared to death. I had no idea that letting out a fart was going to spook the cows like that."

Pearl leaned back in her chair and laughed till Avery thought her sides might split. Then she tooted, of all things, making the other women at the dinner table howl.

Avery buried her head hands, hardly believing her ears. Who were these people, anyway, with their coarse jokes and raucous sense of humor? And who had her mother suddenly become when she met them? It was as if someone ripped open the veil to a part of Pearl's personality Avery hadn't seen in years, if ever.

"What happened next?" Pearl managed to sputter between chuckles.

"Well, Granny T. came to my rescue. She stepped right up

to that oncoming herd and dipped her hand into her pocket to throw some fairy slipper petals at them. Then she stared them down like there was hell to pay if they dared to cross her. Sakes alive, that did the trick—in no time at all, the whole herd turned and made a run for the woods."

"You must have some stare," Avery remarked, only to see Evangeline train her gray, timber-wolf eyes with snippets of yellow on her, sending shivers down her spine. Avery held back a gasp and pretended to cough. "So tell me, what's a fairy slipper?" she said, attempting to change the subject.

"Why, it's an aphrodisiac, honey!" Jubilee piped up. "Granny T.'s the reason my herd increased by a third that year. I swear you could see the trees in the woods shaking with the way those cows carried on."

Avery blushed as red as a stoplight. She shot a glance at Grant at the end of the table, carving more slices of roast beef to serve for seconds with mashed potatoes. He gave Avery a smirk at his grandmother's unbridled humor and slid another plate of roast beef her way.

"I come out to visit Jubilee and gather herbs and wildflowers once or twice a year," Evangeline mentioned, taking a bite of her green beans. "Ever since that day with the cattle," she smiled knowingly, revealing her gold front tooth, "Jubilee's had no trouble keeping the largest herd in the county. It was the least I could do." She gave her friend a wink.

"Herbs and wildflowers? Why do you collect them?" Avery asked.

Evangeline dug into her dress pocket and set a small vial on the table. The lavender fairy slipper petals quivered inside. "Let's just say, I find them rather…useful," she replied. "This flower, for example, only grows in the Rocky Mountains during the summer solstice. I find other things here in winter, too, that prove…worthwhile."

"I know!" Pearl burst excitedly. She pointed at Grant, who was chewing a hefty helping of roast beef and adding au jus to his mashed potatoes. "That's when I met him, in December ten years ago. I was walking in the woods beyond this ranch, looking for boughs for a wreath. I took a trail past a grove of trees that grew really thick, perfect for Christmas decorations. And there he was, like a ghost—rising from the steam of some old spring. I was so shook up it about made me faint. He seemed surprised to see me, too. Then he told me Emmett wasn't gone at all…"

Avery sank back in her chair, thoroughly drained by her mother's babbling, which was more than predictable. She didn't have the gumption to check Grant's reaction this time. Surely he could see now that her mother had mental troubles, and this dinner with strangers—though well meaning—was far too much of a strain.

"Mom," she said gently, cutting her mother's story short with a pat on the hand, "maybe it's time for us to go."

"You'll do no such thing!" ordered Jubilee. "I don't care if we're as full as ticks around this table. No one leaves till they've had my thimbleberry pie. So you two skedaddle," she commanded Grant and Avery, "and go feed the cows before nightfall. By the time you come back we should all be ready for dessert. In the meantime, Granny T. and Miss Pearl will share a cup of tea with me. Ain't that right, ladies?"

"Sounds wonderful!" Pearl clasped her hands together. Her smile stretched from ear to ear, making Avery wince. She didn't have the heart to tear her mother away just yet. The minute they finished their pie later that evening, and this whole dinner debacle was finally over, she swore inside they were leaving as fast as humanly possible.

"We'll have some fresh coffee when you get back as well," Jubilee added, "if that's what you favor. Now get along you two, before it gets dark out there."

Avery shook her head and stole a glance at Grant, relenting with a sigh. She carefully folded her napkin and left it on the table, then collected her plate and silverware and got up, heading for the kitchen behind Grant. When she set her plate beside the sink, Grant picked out two dusters from the wooden pegs by the door. "Would you like a coat?" he offered, holding one up that was frayed at the collar and cuffs. Avery shrugged and put it on, feeling the dirt and hay inside the pockets that reminded of the days when she used to help her dad with cattle. They gave the women a wave and stepped out the door to head for the barn and corrals. Despite her anxiety over her mother, Avery was struck by the vibrant scarlets and tangerines of the sunset on the horizon, casting a warm, tawny glow over the ranch.

"I-I need to apologize," she admitted, "for, you know, the way my mom talked back there. She just gets a little disoriented sometimes, and being around new people is probably too much for her."

"What do you mean, too much?" Grant said, scanning the condition of the fences that rimmed the property. "She seemed perfectly clear-minded to me."

"Nothing's clearer than crazy," Avery replied sadly. "In case you didn't notice, my mom's the most certain person on earth. It's just that what she says doesn't make rational sense. There's *no way* she could have met you ten years ago. Think about it—you would have been a teenager then and wouldn't look like you do now. But she doesn't think about those things. She keeps clinging to her weird fantasy."

Grant turned to Avery, the sunset hues highlighting his chiseled face and making a beautiful amber light glimmer in his blue eyes. He was so handsome in that moment she had to swallow back her reaction, trying hard not to let on that he took her breath away.

"Your dad's accident must have scarred her," he said with understanding in his tone. "Maybe the details afterwards got scattered."

"Scattered? Try downright fictional," Avery replied. "I told you my dad died in a rodeo event. But my mom keeps thinking she saw, well, some kind of messenger afterwards in those woods over there." She pointed to a dark stand of trees flecked with gold from the setting sun.

"Messenger?" Grant said.

"A ghost, I guess you could call it," Avery admitted. "Who apparently looked like…you. That's why she's convinced she's met you before."

"Hmm," Grant surveyed the outline of the nearby forest. "Well, I'm sure you've heard of the legend of Virgil Hollow and Evangeline Tinker? A famous outlaw couple who folks around here say could travel through time."

"Your ancestor, right?"

Grant nodded. "Has it ever occurred to you that maybe your mom really *did* stumble across something?"

"Why do you always take her side?" Avery replied,

frustrated. "Can't you see she's confused? She carries around my Dad's photo and talks to it like she thinks he's coming back, for Christ's sake."

Grant arched a brow, the irony not lost on him. "Obsessed with photos, huh? Not unlike somebody else I know."

Avery stood in her tracks, her hands perched on her hips. "What do you mean?" she demanded.

"Might you be taking pictures of cowboys for the same reason?"

"I do it as a viable *business*." She glared at him. "Because it earns me a hell of a lot of money."

"Which you need to take care of your mom in a nice hotel instead of some institution, right?" Grant leaned closer to Avery, making her heart skip. His eyes were dead serious, but with a deep empathy that made her insides twist, like perhaps he actually cared. "You're damn amazing, Avery Smart," he finally said in a low tone. "You've been on your own since you were a teen, stepping up to the plate and looking after your mom, no matter how bad the cards were that life dealt. But let's face it, there are a lot of other ways to make money. Selling stocks, dealing in real estate—and a woman like you certainly could have been a top model."

Avery clasped her hands and twisted her fingers, praying her self-consciousness didn't show.

"But of all things," Grant continued, "you chose to specialize in cowboy photos?"

"Okay Sigmund Freud," she defended, "it doesn't take a genius to figure out that maybe I wasn't ready to let go of my dad, either." Tears surfaced in Avery's eyes, which she fought to blink back. "But I'm not exactly putting you on the couch right now."

"Wouldn't mind if you did," Grant replied with an easy smile. "There's a nice soft stack of hay in the barn, too."

His words made Avery blush. She sucked in a breath to pull herself together. "It's just that my mom needs help, not some cheerleader to feed her fantasies."

"Are you sure she's the one who needs help?"

"Huh?"

Grant folded his broad arms and gazed out over the ranch, watching the silhouettes of the cows slowly falling in line to head for the barn.

"You're mom's happy, Avery. Especially when you let her get some sunshine and socialize. You and I both know those ladies are in the homestead right now telling off-color jokes and laughing it up over thimbleberry pie. I wouldn't be surprised if they've broken into my grandma's homemade wine." He turned and stared at Avery with a piercing gaze. "I hate to say it, but *you're* the one who's not having any fun. Look around. Most folks would call this view breathtaking. You've been wearing a frown the whole time."

Avery's mouth dropped. She glanced around the Lazy C Ranch. He was right—the landscape was utterly gorgeous, marked by towering mountains tinted a rosy-lavender hue from the dipping sun and flanked by dark woods on either side.

"Well, maybe this is my happy face," she rationalized. "I am a business woman, you know—I have to be tough."

"Or maybe it's the face you've bravely worn since your dad died."

To Avery's astonishment, Grant's lips pressed against hers in a bold, stolen kiss. He gently clutched her shoulders and pulled her toward him, working her lips long and slow. Then his hands cupped her cheeks as he kept drinking her in as if she were as golden as the sunset.

"You're beautiful, Avery," he said, breaking away and stroking her cheeks with his thumbs. "I'd like to change that face. To see it smile more often."

Part of Avery wanted to run. To storm to the ranch house and grab her mother and go back to exactly the way things were—safe and secure, with her mother's photos of her dad all over the hotel room walls and her career in full swing, snapping photos of two-dimensional cowboys.

But here was a real, flesh and blood cowboy, one who'd kissed her and told her she was beautiful, igniting sparks that snapped all over skin and made wild sensations riddle through her body, scaring the crap out of her. Avery held her breath for a moment and dared to look into Grant's eyes.

In those eyes were pure blue flames—a look of such yearning and sincerity that it made Avery gasp. She'd spent her whole career looking for a cowboy that perfect to sell in pictures. And here he was, right in front of her, staring at her like he was for keeps. But was it all an illusion? Like her mother's peculiar fantasies?

Grant didn't say a word. He simply swept the copper hair away from Avery's forehead, his hand lingering on her temple. It felt warm and strong.

"Y-You shouldn't have done that," Avery sputtered, clenching her jaw to keep herself from lunging for another kiss.

"Why not?" Grant brazenly swiped another kiss and smiled. "Because you can't control me with your lens?"

"No," Avery said too fast. "Because any fool knows cowboys aren't forever. They always leave."

Grant's eyes narrowed, the warm sunset tones highlighting their turquoise blue. "And pictures *don't*? My God, do you hear yourself, Avery? I'm standing in front of you, my feet planted in the dirt of my family's homestead, and I'm not going anywhere. The Hollows may have their outlaw tendencies, but they've been here for generations. This fricking town was named after them. Are you telling me you're stuck on repeat like your mom, all because your dad died in a freak accident—doing what he loved?"

Avery took a step back as though she'd been shaken awake for the first time in years.

Grant grabbed her and kissed her again, hard. When he was finally out of breath, he let go. "What does it take to prove to you that some cowboys stay?" he said.

"Staying," she replied.

A wicked grin pulled at Grant's lips. "You're on, pretty lady," he said with a glint in his eye. "Because this is one cowboy who loves nothing better than a challenge. But there's one thing I want in return—besides more kisses, of course."

Avery bit her lip, bracing for his reply. Was she really having this conversation? With a drop-dead handsome cowboy about kisses and forevers at sunset? Or was she making some kind of crazy deal with the devil right now? The whole situation felt way too far out of control. And the damnedest thing was, something deep inside her heart was beginning to like it.

"I want to take your picture tonight," Grant said. "In the moonlight, so I can see the way your eyes looks under the stars."

Avery struggled for breath. God as her witness, that was the sexiest thing a man had ever said to her. Taking only second place to the penetrating look right now in Grant's amazing blue eyes.

"Why would you want to do that?" she asked.

Grant linked his arm in hers and began to walk in the direction of the lowing cows near the barn, impatient for dinner. "Because, Avery," he said, "I want something of you that lasts forever, too."

Avery slipped her hand into her pocket, reeling from the impact of his words, when she felt something long and slim with her fingers. She stroked its silky texture for a moment and pulled it out, holding it up to the dim sunlight.

It was a fairy slipper petal.

And it was trembling.

13

Jubilee's mouth was pressed into a firm line as she poured Pearl and Evangeline cups of tea. She set the teapot down on a trivet on the dining room table, then looked Pearl square in the eye.

"Honey," she stated in a grave tone, "what you saw ten years ago in the woods near here was no fantasy. That man was Virgil Hollow."

Pearl glanced up from her plate of thimbleberry pie. She dropper her fork, making a clatter.

"Th-The legend? You mean it's *real?*" She turned and squinted at Evangeline, then cast her gaze to the sepia-toned wanted poster on the wall. "Oh my Lord," she gasped, "you're Evangeline Tinker!" She waved her hands frantically, making her wheeze. "Oh, it's such an honor to meet you! I don't know why he appeared to me that day, but when I stumbled across him, he said, 'He's not gone. He's waiting for you.'"

"There-there now, dear," Evangeline said, pushing a honey

pot toward her for her tea. "I'll bet the moon was full that night—the Cold Moon near the winter solstice. Ain't that right?"

Pearl thought back for a second, her eyes growing wide. "Wait a minute—that's true! How on earth did you know?"

Evangeline took a sip of her tea and nodded. "Because he was waiting for *me*, sweetie. Every December, under the Cold Moon, we visit with each other. You just beat me to the... portal...next to the hot spring that night. So out of mercy, he gave you a little information from the other side. My Virgil has a big heart that way."

"See honey," Jubilee confirmed, "you never were crazy. I don't understand it half the time either, but Evangeline comes from a long line of Travelers who have secrets most folks wouldn't believe. The only reason I know is because I saw him too, when I was ten years old. Me and Evangeline have been friends ever since." She gazed at Pearl with conviction in her eyes. "Everything you've heard about Virgil and Evangeline is real. You and I are the only ones who know the truth about the portal near the Lazy C Ranch."

"But if he can visit her from 1895, and she can visit him from the present, why don't they stick together all the time?" Pearl asked. "I'd give my eyeteeth to be with Emmett again—"

"Sometimes you can love someone so much," Evangeline broke in with a somber tone, "that it'll be the death of you, darlin'. Yet you can't bear to be rid of that person, either. Such love is magical and eternal, beyond human understandin'. My Virgil was as an outlaw, honey. It was only a matter of time before he got shot through the chest. I couldn't change him if I tried—and to be honest, I didn't want to. But I couldn't stop loving him, or watch him die either. So I came back to my time. We made a lover's pact to visit."

"D-Does he know? I mean, your grandson that looks just like him—"

"Grant knows about the legend. That's all."

"She was a young, naive woman," Jubilee added, "when she went back in time looking for extinct herbs, and met Virgil Hollow." She glanced at the wanted poster of them on the wall. "She didn't know a love like that would last forever."

"You were beautiful," Pearl said, stealing a timid look at Evangeline's extraordinary features. "The most beautiful woman I've ever seen. Still are."

"Thank you kindly," Evangeline replied, narrowing her spooky eyes. "Now, I do believe we need to go to the portal tonight—he'll want to see you."

"Who?"

"You know who."

Pearl's eyes grew wide, and so did Jubilee's.

"C-Can you do that?" Pearl pressed. "Can you bring us together, like Virgil said way back then?"

Evangeline nodded slowly, making Jubilee gasp.

"But they're ordinary folks, Evangeline!" Jubilee protested. "Not like you. We don't know how the magic will—"

"Nobody ever knows, till they try." Granny's lips curled into a crooked smile. "No guts, no glory, right?"

"What about my daughter?" Pearl said. "She'll want to see him, too." Pearl met Jubilee's gaze, whose eyes looked as uncertain as she felt.

Granny nodded at the window behind Pearl, revealing the last traces of a sunset. "That's up to her. 'Tis a fact of human

87

nature that folks only see what they want to see, when they're ready. I could light myself on fire in the middle of a fairy ring, and a gal like Avery might not blink an eye."

Pearl chuckled a little. "That's my Avery—you certainly pegged her right. She's a tough one. Had to be, with everything that happened in our lives. I know the reason she's so driven is on account of me. She takes care of everything."

Evangeline's eyes glinted. "Anybody could tell that just by lookin' at her, with that firm jaw and those stern eyes. But I also know ain't none of that gonna matter."

Pearl looked at her, puzzled.

Evangeline stared through the window at Grant and Avery ambling slowly back toward the homestead, outlined by the fading glow of the sunset.

"'Cause she's already started to fall in love with him, even if she can't admit it yet. But I will let you in on a little tip—my fairy slipper petals don't work unless the person secretly wants them to. So don't you worry none, Pearl," Evangeline said, easing her fears. "I happen to know from personal experience that when a Hollow man gives his heart, it's forever." Her lips lifted at the corners a little. "Now let's hurry up and have another piece of pie."

14

The minute Avery and Grant stepped through the door, Shae began blowing up Avery's cell phone. "It's raining men!" she texted in a flurry, including a selfie of her country line dancing at the Outlaw's Hideout Bar and Grill in town with a group of good-looking cowboys. "I've already passed out all the photography waivers I have! We've got more than enough cowboys to meet our deadline. This calendar's going to be a snap! You just relax tonight with whatever you're doing. We can fit in more photography shoots tomorrow."

Avery smiled, admiring Shae's exuberance.

"You ready for a moonlight ride?" Jubilee asked Avery and Grant before they could hang up their coats. She shot a glance at Evangeline and Pearl to confirm their secret plan. "It would be nice to get in Grant's ol' truck and, um, show Pearl the moon and stars over the Lazy C Ranch. What do you think?"

"Hmm, that's interesting," Avery noted, checking Grant's

reaction. "We were just talking about taking a few moonlight photos."

"As long as we get dessert afterwards," Grant insisted, eyeing the thimbleberry pie. "You did promise, remember?"

"With vanilla ice cream on top!" Jubilee assured him, rising from her seat. "C'mon, Pearl and Evangeline—let's grab a few quilts from my closets to lay in the truck bed to keep us warm. I swear, you won't *believe* how beautiful this ranch looks under the stars. We'll meet you out front in a few minutes, Grant."

By the time the three women walked out of the homestead with piles of quilts in their arms, Grant had already gone into the barn and fetched a battery-operated space heater to put in the back of his truck to help keep the ladies warm. He pulled the truck up to the front door and hopped out, ready to help them climb into the bed. When the ladies were nestled inside on top of their soft quilts, he motioned for Avery to join him in the cab.

"Wow, this ranch really does look different at night," Avery remarked as he pulled forward, clicking her seat belt and setting her camera on the seat. "The trees take on a silvery hue in the moonlight. Is that the effect you were hoping for?"

"Any photo of you is fine by me," Grant replied, gently stepping on the gas. They proceeded to drive on a dirt road that led over rolling hills of pasture. Then they wound past trees and meadows, until Grant heard a knock on his back window. He slowly halted the truck and let it idle, opening the glass behind him to see his grandmother's face.

"Hey sweetie, would you mind veering right down that road that leads to the stand of woods beyond the ranch?" Jubilee asked. "I'd love to see the way the moonlight glimmers through those old-growth trees. When I was a little girl, I used to explore that area all the time. But be careful—don't be running over any fairy slippers."

"Uh, okay," Grant said, a bit taken aback by her request. "I guess for nostalgia's sake, to the grove of trees we go."

He headed right and steered down the dirt road until his headlights met an old gate, indicating the edge of the Lazy C Ranch. Grant hopped out to unlock the gate and climbed back in the truck. Pressing the gas pedal, he proceeded with caution, respecting his grandmother's wishes in case there were any wildflowers. After about half a mile, when the road finally leveled out near a grassy area surrounded by tall, old-growth trees, he brought the truck to a stop.

"This looks good," he said to Avery, turning off the ignition. His eyes told her he already enjoyed the way the moonlight caressed her checks and lips. Grabbing her camera, Grant gave her a quick smile as they stepped of the truck.

"Goodness, this is beautiful!" gasped Pearl in the truck bed, clutching a quilt up to her chin.

"You too cold to walk around, Mom?" asked Avery. "We can head back whenever you like. I don't want you to get tired."

"No-no," she replied, sneaking a look Evangeline's way. "I can't wait to see those old trees Jubilee was talking about. She said they're ponderosas and have been here over four-hundred years."

Avery and Grant carefully helped the women out of the back of the truck, watching their neck's crane at the beauty of the starry night sky, where every constellation seemed impossibly close. To their surprise, they noticed Jubilee pulling out a bottle of her homemade, thimbleberry wine and a stack of old teacups from beneath a quilt she carried. She spread the quilt over a grassy spot and proceeded to pour each person a cup, setting down her bottle. All the while, Grant confidently snapped Avery's picture, her hair and features rimmed in platinum by the rising full moon. It was so bright out that it wasn't hard to see, and the group stepped easily around rocks and twigs that might normally make them stumble.

As Jubilee handed Avery a vintage teacup, the call of a great horned owl peeled through the night, startling her. Goosebumps ran down her skin while the sound echoed through the trees. She squinted, spying a curl of mist rising over the nearby woods. Then she lifted the teacup to her lips. The rich, thimbleberry flavor was heavy and sweet with just a hint of sharpness, almost like a port. She nudged Grant and pointed at the dark stand of trees. "Did you see that mist? There must be some kind of spring over there," she observed. "The vapor looks silvery in the moonlight." She turned to Pearl, holding her finger in that direction. "See, Mom?"

A column of mist rose to the moon, making gentle swirls in the night sky. Curious, Grant snapped a few pictures, then hooked his arm through Avery's and began to walk toward it. The women followed after them with their teacups of wine in tow. Stepping carefully around logs and boulders, they reached an opening in a ponderosa grove. Little tufts of steam rose over a thin stream that bubbled from of the earth.

"It's an old hot spring," Jubilee said, nodding at the way the moonlight glinted off the warm water. Curiously, the steam began to fan out in a wider haze, almost like a gray curtain. Before they knew it, a shadowy figure arose in the mist.

Astonished, Grant took several photos, when the shutter suddenly stopped working.

Dimensions of the figure became clearer, revealing the chiseled face of a tall man wearing a black hat and old-fashioned, nineteenth-century clothes. Though his hair was laced with silver, he looked just like…

Grant Hollow—

Pearl dropped her teacup to the ground with a crash.

"It's him!" she cried, swiveling to Avery. "I told you all along he was real! These women believed me—they brought us here to see. That's none other than Virgil Hollow!"

Speechless, Avery was too stunned to utter a word. Her wide eyes were glued to the man in the mist, when she saw him reach out his hand toward Pearl.

"He's not gone," he said kindly. "He's waiting for you."

At that moment, Avery saw her father appear behind Virgil, knocking the breath out of her. Emmett smiled in that familiar crooked way she remembered from childhood, his light brown hair disheveled, with those warm creases she always loved near his eyes. He looked just like he did on that fateful morning when he headed for the Outlaw Days Rodeo for his final ride. Avery began to shake all over, leaning on Grant for support.

"Daddy?" she gasped. She saw her mother drop the quilt she'd wrapped around herself and proceed toward him with surprisingly eager steps. "Wait—Mom, what the hell are you doing?"

Evangeline stepped up and laid a hand on Avery's shoulder. She squeezed hard.

"Let her go, child," she warned. "Pearl needs this."

"Needs what?" Avery retorted. "Is this some group hallucination or something?" She lifted her teacup to Evangeline with wild accusation in her eyes. "What on earth did you and Jubilee put in this wine?"

Evangeline released one of her loud, eerie cackles that set the whole forest on edge. Avery swore it shook the trees.

"It ain't the wine, darlin'," Evangeline replied mysteriously. "It's the heart. Someday you'll understand. But for now, my Virgil's simply doing her a favor."

Avery shook her head, her heart racing. She had no idea what this crazy old bat was talking about. All she could do was grip Grant's arm tighter, watching her mother step into the misty veil. Sobs choked in Avery's throat as her parents appeared to give each other a tight hug, becoming one shady column in the haze.

"What's happening?" Avery burst. "Is she coming back? Mom?" She pressed, reaching out her arms. "Mom!"

"Let her go, honey," Jubilee warned, joining Evangeline beside Grant and Avery. "This is for your mother to decide, not us."

At that moment, the figure of Virgil Hollow nodded at Evangeline with a smile as wide as the sky as he began to recede in the mist. Avery's parents, whose outlines she could only see in hazy gray tones as if they'd become phantoms, appeared to become entwined. For the life of her, Avery thought she saw them kiss.

"Don't it touch your heart," Evangeline said, her silver hair glowing in the moonlight. To everyone's surprise, Pearl broke free from her husband's grasp, her image becoming clearer. She turned and looked at the group in front of her for a long time, as if weighing her future. Then she stepped boldly out of the mist, walking with more confident strides than Avery had ever seen.

At that moment, a star fell from the sky.

Avery ran to Pearl and wrapped her arms around her so tightly she nearly squeezed the breath out of her.

"Mom! What happened? Was that…Daddy? What did he say?"

Pearl reached up and grasped her daughter's cheeks, peering into her eyes.

"He said live your life, honey. Do what you love most. It's only a matter of time till we're together again. Then he told me a little secret."

"S-Secret?" Avery sputtered, tears spilling down her cheeks. She didn't know, quite frankly, if she could take any more secrets at this point.

"He said time don't mean a thing," Pearl said softly. "Only the heart."

"Lord have mercy," Jubilee said, turning to Evangeline and elbowing her. "That's the most beautiful thing I ever heard! So why don't we share a toast and head on back to the homestead?" She gave Evangeline a harder nudge, handing her the bottle of wine to pour. While Grant and Avery lifted their eyes to the constellations one last time, Evangeline reached into her pocket and sprinkled a powder into the wine bottle, making the liquid glisten in the moonlight. Then she refilled Grant's and Avery's cups, discretely leaving out Jubilee's and Pearl's.

"Wow," said Grant to Avery, after they'd both taken a sip,

"that's one hearty wine. Kinda makes me yearn for pie, too. You ready to head back?"

"Sure," replied Avery, indulging in another sip. For some reason, she became a little disoriented, forgetting why they'd stopped at this particular spot. Then she noticed her camera around Grant's neck, recalling that he'd wanted to try taking night pictures. "Hope your moonlight photos turn out well," she remarked, gazing again at the stars. She clinked her teacup against Grant's. "It sure is a beautiful night."

15

Avery sat on her couch next to Grant, scanning the photos she'd printed earlier that day in her darkroom studio. One in particular held her interest: it was a night shot Grant had taken outside the Lazy C Ranch near a grove of trees two weeks ago. The picture appeared rather hazy with what looked like a figure in the silvery mist. Avery felt drawn to the photo, but she couldn't quite articulate why.

Then she picked up a nearby newspaper that featured a picture of her mother, smiling broadly in a small headshot on the front page. The blurb beneath it stated that Pearl Smart had won nearly three-hundred dollars at the Bootjack Casino near Bandits Hollow, after a birthday bash thrown for her by friends.

Friends—

Oddly enough, the word stung Avery's heart a little. Ever since that night when her mother had gone for a moonlight ride on the Lazy C Ranch, for some reason, she no longer clung to her father's photo anymore. Most of the time, she could be found galavanting with Jubilee and Evangeline at flea markets, bingo parlors, even dancing it up late at night at the Outlaw's Hideout Bar and Grill. Pearl had become so active and self-sufficient she didn't require June to look after her anymore, and Avery was forced to let her go. It was as if her mother had become a new woman.

Avery carefully folded the newspaper and set it down, turning to Grant.

"Being my mom's caretaker has been my focus my whole adult life," she confessed, her voice stumbling a little. "I'm so happy she has friends now. But I hardly know who I am if I'm not looking after her."

"I'd love to help you find out," Grant replied. He leaned over and rubbed her cheek softly.

"Seriously—a rodeo man? Who travels from event to event, living on the road?"

Grant shook his head. "Nope. Building up my grandma's ranch to its original glory and raising grass-fed cattle for the organic beef market. Maybe buffalo, too. I need new challenges, Avery." He picked up a stack of photos from the coffee table and pulled out one he'd taken of her in the woods a fortnight ago under the moonlight, holding it up. The pale light over Avery's features made her look lovely and ethereal, like a fairy princess. "Including courting an amazing photographer who's only begun to explore her talent—and her life. What do you say, Avery? After the bull riding tour ends in November, I want to see what else I can do. Now that you're no longer preoccupied with your mom, maybe you can explore new things, too."

"You mean, you're going to retire?"

"No. I mean I'm setting out on whole new adventures."

He slipped on top of her and cradled her lap with his thick legs, staring into her eyes. Then he clutched her face and gave her a long, passionate kiss. A forever kind of kiss, and it left her reeling.

"What do you think, Avery?" he said, breaking away. "You ready to see what the rest of life holds?"

Avery eyes fluttered, still reveling in the sweet sensation of his lips. She gazed at the other prints spread across her coffee table, including the two-dimensional photos she'd taken of cowboys for the upcoming calendar. The shots were spectacular, each man sexy beyond belief with that trademark sincerity in his eyes befitting a My Forever Cowboy. But none of them belonged to her. They were strangers.

Avery lifted her chin and planted another kiss on the very real cowboy in front of her, whose eyes were so blue they looked like they could peer into infinity. The soft, expectant expression on Grant's face confirmed what she'd suspected for a while: when a man in the Hollow family falls for a woman, he gives his heart for keeps.

"Well, Grant," she said, "I don't see why your new adventures and my new adventures can't coincide," she smiled with a sparkle in her eye. She glanced at the interlocking circles tattooed on his forearm, tracing her finger along the permanent blue lines that connected with each other in rings, spiraling over and over again. "Who knows where those adventures could take us. Or if they might lead to—"

"Forever?" Grant cut in before he pressed his lips to hers for another kiss. He bowed his forehead against Avery's and laced his hands through her fingers, locking them together. Then he clutched them tight and gazed into her eyes.

"When it comes to forever, Avery," Grant said, "my bet's on you."

Avery smiled, simply drinking in his gorgeous face. Then she loosened her hand from his grip and wriggled her fingers into her front jeans pocket, pulling out the fairy slipper petal she'd found two weeks ago. It was dried and crinkled now, yet still tinged with a slight lavender hue.

"Tell me something," she asked Grant. "Do you think Granny T. might have cast a spell on us? She's pretty spooky, you know. And I found this fairy slipper petal in the duster pocket I wore on our moonlight walk. It's supposed to be an aphrodisiac."

Grant's lips lifted in a smile. "Well, I overheard my grandma confiding to a friend that fairy slippers don't work unless you want them to. So why don't we find out?" He gave her a kiss with a gleam in his eye. "Let our new adventures begin."

ALSO BY DIANE J. REED

On a clear winter night, the Cold Moon shines a light that illuminates the past...

Travel back in time to meet Virgil Hollow, Iron Feather, and the Bandits Hollow Gang.

Buy now!

DISCOVER THE IRON FEATHER BROTHERS

They're tough, dangerous, and family means everything.

A contemporary western romance series with strong men, and even stronger women.

Buy now!

ABOUT THE AUTHOR

USA TODAY bestselling author Diane J. Reed writes happily ever afters with a touch of magic that make you believe in the power of love. Her stories feed the soul with outlaws, mavericks, and dreamers who have big hearts under big skies and dare to risk all for those they cherish. Because love is more than a feeling—it's the magic that changes everything.

To get the latest on new releases, sign up for Diane J. Reed's newsletter at dianejreed.com.

CPSIA information can be obtained
at www.ICGtesting.com
Printed in the USA
FSHW011254230721
83505FS